The Picture Island

The Picture Island

Michael S. Manley

Illustrations by
Marta Maszkiewicz

Halo
PUBLISHING
INTERNATIONAL

Halo Publishing International
7550 W IH-10 #800, PMB 2069,
San Antonio, TX 78229

First Edition, November 2024
ISBN: 978-1-63765-662-4
Library of Congress Control Number: 2024915165

Halo Publishing International is a self-publishing company that publishes adult fiction and non-fiction, children's literature, self-help, spiritual, and faith-based books. We continually strive to help authors reach their publishing goals and provide many different services that help them do so. We do not publish books that are deemed to be politically, religiously, or socially disrespectful, or books that are sexually provocative, including erotica. Halo reserves the right to refuse publication of any manuscript if it is deemed not to be in line with our principles. Do you have a book idea you would like us to consider publishing? Please visit www.halopublishing.com for more information.

For David, John, Anna, Emile, Kevin, and Amy—
Merry Christmas.

And for Mom and Dad, who never cared
when the math was not in my favor.

CONTENTS

CHAPTER ONE

Miss Bunion

F ar down a crooked lane lined with tall trees, which hid it from the world, sat the Hortense P. Bunion Home for Extra Children. Like too many of its current residents, it was sad and neglected. The ivy leaves that crept up the brick walls of the large house had fallen away weeks before, leaving only wan, brittle tendrils snaking up like a hundred insect legs in search of a body. The copper roof, with its sharply pointed gables, was now, from years of wind and rain, the color of a gargoyle's tongue. Snow a foot deep covered the ground—but there were no sled tracks or snowmen on this land, merely stacks and stacks of firewood. Playtime, you see, was not looked upon kindly by Miss Bunion, for it stirred the minds of children and was—in her mind—a detriment to work. And to Miss Bunion, work was the truest virtue—the sooner a child learned that, the better.

And learn they did. Gathering wood, sweeping floors, cleaning dishes, scrubbing soot—work that dulled the spark of wonder and killed hope. Work that, day in and day out, left the imagination a cold, empty room whose windows were shuttered and doors bolted as if for a storm—work that kept out only dreams.

Extra children. Twenty-seven now live here, each of them surplus—a mouth too many for mothers and fathers going hungry themselves. Some of them had been left on church steps as babies; one had been wrapped neatly and left in the garbage bin. Every so often there were visitors to the Bunion Home, but there was little hope any of the extra children would be adopted—Miss Bunion saw to that herself.

"Aren't you a sweet little girl," a possible mother once said of six-year old Sally.

"Humph," Miss Bunion interrupted, "she is feeble and dull-witted. Who would want such a child?"

And so it would be, for all of them, until the possible mother or father left in despair.

Most of the children spent their entire young lives at the Bunion Home, until the time when they were old enough to be sent off to work in the factory. You see, Miss Bunion had a cousin, a Mr. Grundy Bunion, whose business it was to salvage used staples, melt them down, and reform the metal into paper clips. Any unclaimed, extra children were sent to work in the factory at the age of fifteen, often remaining employees of the Bunion Fastener Reclamation and Foundry, Inc. until the day they died. And if Miss Bunion profited over the years from providing her cousin with a steady supply of cheap labor, no one—save she and Grundy Bunion—was ever the wiser.

* * *

"Very well then, I shall bless the food," said Miss Bunion as the extra children stared hopelessly at their breakfast plates.

Of all the unpleasant things at the Bunion Home for Extra Children—the spiders making their peculiar lace under beds, or the bats swooping through the chimney and hanging in the coat closet on cold nights— it was Miss Bunion herself whom the children dreaded most of all. Tall and thin with gray, crinkled wasp-nest skin under a head of swooping cotton-candy hair—if cotton candy came in the flavor of dust—Miss Bunion had to be at least one hundred years old. There were even stories whispered between the bunks that she was a witch who would live forever. Of that, we cannot be certain, but there could be no mistake about her opinion of children—Miss Bunion hated children more than anything else in the world.

This morning was no different from the last, or any other as far back as the children could remember. They had assembled in the great dining room, taken their places on hard wooden benches, and silently dreamed of warm pancakes, smoked sausages, and scrambled eggs. Oh, how they dreamed of such food! But today was no different, as we have said before, and in came Ursa, the cook, pulling a vat with one hand and wielding her ladle in the other. And then the sound—oh, the sound!—the awful, sticky *plop* as Ursa flung a lumpy white mass into each child's bowl. It was a sound pancakes were too polite to make, a sound sausage would find unthinkable.

When everyone had been served, Miss Bunion began. And like depressed robots, the children made themselves say the blessing with her:

> *God bless this mess.*
> *Hair it will put on my chest.*
> *Eat it all; that's the test.*
> *Pray it doesn't knock me dead.*

This was followed by the sound of twenty-seven spoons, in twenty-seven bowls, hitting the pasty skin of the cold, gray, utterly flavorless mound of Irish oatmeal before them.

"I do despise the sight of a hungry child, Ursa," remarked Miss Bunion. Indeed, Miss Bunion despised the sight of all children, regardless of whether they were hungry or full.

"Time for the juice then," replied Ursa as she lumbered her three-hundred-pound self back into the kitchen. On the way, she saw a question sparking in the eyes of little Sally, who had not yet given up all hope. "Sorry, little one, potato again today," she whispered.

Sally's face lost all of its shine, replaced with an ashen veil. Small for her age, Sally was one of the few who managed to dream in a place where so many dreams had died from hunger and neglect.

"Don't be sad," said Ant, who sat next to her. "We'll make do—like always, eh?" Ant, a boy of eight, had been left in a basket next to a mailbox. The short note attached to the basket said, "PLEASE TAKE CARE OF OUR SON ANT"—here the ink had been washed away by the rain, erasing the rest of his name—"HOPE HE'S NOT TOO MUCH TROUBLE, THANKS A BUNCH."

"Yes," sighed Sally, "we'll make do, like always."

And then twenty-seven sad little faces hunched over twenty-seven sad gray plates, eyes staring at their breakfast of Irish oatmeal and potato juice. No, this morning was not any different from the last, or the one before that.

Yet, very soon, for Sally and Ant at least, the Hortense P. Bunion Home for Extra Children would be but a memory.

CHAPTER TWO

The Boy with a Horn

In another time, and far across the sea from the Bunion Home for Extra Children, lived a fisherman and his wife. More than anything else in the world, they wanted a child of their own. Each day, the fisherman rowed out and caught boatloads of fish that he sold at the market, and each day the fisherman's wife knitted caps and booties for the little baby they knew would someday come.

"Five bass and two prickly eels," the fisherman would say when he came back from a long day on the ocean.

"Two ear socks and a cap," the fisherman's wife would reply, tallying what she had knitted that day.

"God, if you smiled on me and blessed me with a baby, I would be so happy," prayed the fisherman's wife every morning and every night.

"God, if you smiled on me and blessed me with a son, I would be so happy," prayed the fisherman as he rowed out every morning and back every night.

One day, God smiled, and that is how little Bucky came into the world.

* * *

"Well?" scowled the fisherman after a long and stormy day at sea. "Any change?"

The fisherman's wife shook her head and continued rocking their new baby to sleep.

"Humph," said the fisherman, filling a cup with day-old coffee. It had been two weeks since the baby was born, and the fisherman was bothered by the triangular shape little Bucky's head was taking. Indeed, it seemed to grow more triangular every day.

"Perfectly fine otherwise," offered the fisherman's wife hopefully. "Just a bit…different, is all."

"Pointy," grunted the fisherman as he squinted at the child. "Who ever heard of a pointy baby?"

He scowled and sipped his coffee as his wife sighed and rocked. And little Bucky slept peacefully in her lap, not yet aware of his difference or the world's intolerance for it.

* * *

As the days that passed turned into weeks, they took with them any hope that the boy born to the fisherman and his wife would ever be normal—the triangular bump high on the baby's forehead was now sprouting the unmistakable beginnings of a horn. It was neither curved like a rhino's nor branched like a deer's. Instead, it seemed to spiral straight out and up, pointing to the sky. No one else in their town had ever seen anything like it before, nor could anyone explain the strange phenomenon of a child with a horn growing right out of his head.

And no one much cared to, either. In the market square of their small seaside village, mothers covered their own children's eyes as they passed Bucky, or shooed them away from him. Everyone knew that demons traveled in passing glances, and if ever there lived demons among men, they were certain that they inhabited this deformed, pointy boy.

As Bucky learned to walk, he slouched, and his head hung so that he seemed always to be staring at the ground. Whether this was from the weight of the horn—now almost a foot long—or the shame from others' reactions to it, no one could say. His slouching caused his horn to point more forward and often become an unwitting weapon. This made Bucky a walking accident. He once speared a cabbage as he shuffled through the market. On another walk, he poked the baker's horse and sent the cart of muffins and tarts into the air as the horse reared up and brayed.

"Keep away from that one!" a father shouted to his children while squinting and pointing to Bucky.

"Don't look at him, or he'll turn you into a gargoyle!" a mother warned.

In spite of this, the small fire of life still warmed and lit Bucky's heart—for he knew that beyond this little seaside town, the world was vast and full of possibilities.

* * *

Because he was awkward and because others feared him so, Bucky often lost himself in the town's maritime library. It was the one place where his horn seemed to be an asset—he used it to pull down books that were too high to reach, and he could turn a volume's pages while eating a sardine sandwich with both hands. He loved the weight and feel of books, and though he was too young to read, he was comforted by pictures of animals and sea life more unusual than he. He once saw a picture of an enormous gray creature with a horn coming straight out of its head, much like his own.

His fingers spent hours crossing oceans on the maps of unknown lands, as his eyes danced over the rows of symbols on the pages. "Soon I will go to school," Bucky said to himself, "and it won't matter that I'm not like anyone else...I'll learn how to read and lose myself in the sea of words and pictures in these books until I am one hundred degrees!" Bucky had heard others talking in the library about their degrees, and he naturally thought that all smart people must be very high in temperature.

But the fisherman and his wife were blind to Bucky's dreams—indeed, they were blind to everything about Bucky, save the horn that sprang from his head and their anger with God.

"God, I asked you to smile, but instead you frowned," prayed the fisherman's wife.

"I wanted a boy, but you gave me a freak," complained the fisherman to God.

And this broke God's heart because he saw that the fisherman and his wife could not love. And God never smiled on them again.

CHAPTER THREE

The Stone Room

After their breakfast of Irish oatmeal and potato juice, the children of the Bunion Home set about their assigned chores. Some stayed indoors and cleaned dishes or mopped floors, while others were sent outside to gather kindling. Ant and Sally seized every opportunity to leave the clammy, dark, dreamless halls of the Bunion Home, even on the coldest of days such as this one.

"Ant," Sally began as they walked through the snow toward the woods, "why is Miss Bunion so awful?"

Ant considered this carefully. "Well...I think it's because she's evil."

"Well then, why is she evil?" continued Sally.

Ant had been afraid she might ask that. The question of why Miss Bunion was evil was a puzzle that the child tenants of the Bunion Home had been trying to solve for years. Some thought she was a witch, and others thought she was a vampire queen. But all knew that she hated children for no good reason whatsoever.

"Now, why is Miss Bunion evil," Ant stated the question as if it were the mystery of the universe. "That is the key, isn't it, Sally? For if we knew why Miss Bunion was so evil, we might have a chance."

"A chance for what?"

Ant stopped in his tracks to give weight to his next words. "Why, a chance to get out of here, of course."

Sally looked him straight in the eye to make sure he wasn't fooling her. "You really think so?" she said with wide eyes.

"Maybe…or maybe not. The outcome is…inconclusive." Ant saw Sally's face go gray and her eyes droop. "But, Sally, I know for certain that if you believe, if you truly believe in something with everything you have, then anything is possible."

A sparkle returned to Sally's eyes as she thought this over. "You know something? I believe you, Ant."

Ant was surprised to hear himself reply, "And I believe me too, Sally."

"Shake on it?" said Sally, offering her hand.

Ant took her hand in his. "What are we shaking on?"

"That anything is possible if we believe with everything we have," whispered Sally.

"Deal," said Ant, and they shook three times just to be sure.

Just then, as if by magic, Sally and Ant—who had wandered too far into the woods while talking—found themselves standing in a magnificent stone garden, at the foot of vertical columns of granite that emerged next to a steep outcropping of rock. Near the far edge, they found four perfect chairs, each with high rock backs and wide rock arms. In front of those sat a stone table.

"Oh, Ant, what is it?" cried Sally.

"Those look like big chairs," he said, climbing toward them.

"This looks like a table," said Sally.

"It's a stone room," said Ant, dusting snow off one of the chairs.

"No, Ant, it's a *throne* room!" exclaimed Sally, climbing up to sit next to Ant.

Ant and Sally's coats were worn and thin, and on their feet they wore sad, old moccasins wrapped in burlap. Miss Bunion believed in frugality and economy above all—she saw no need to waste the meager allowance she received for her troubles on clothing for children whom no one wanted. But if Sally and Ant failed to notice the time passing, or the dull chill that was setting in, they could be forgiven, for here they had found something utterly unknown, something magical. And if the stone room that they now explored with such pure pleasure on this winter day was partly or wholly the work of their own imagination, well, they cared not in the slightest. For this was a secret that held magic, and—for a little while, anyway—it was theirs alone.

"Ant! Sally! Where have you been?" It was Penny calling, a thin girl of eleven with long black hair that she hid under a ratty scarf.

"We've been looking for you for hours!" said Buster. He was ten, but acted much older because he was very tall. "You've missed lunch!"

"Come see, come see the throne room we've found!" cried Sally, not at all upset that she had missed another lunch of creamed leaves and oatmeal patties.

"It was left behind by the king," concluded Ant.

Penny and Buster made their way toward Sally and Ant, traipsing over the rocky ground. *Why did they come so far into the woods,* Buster wondered, *when there is kindling so much closer to the Bunion home?*

"Get down from there, both of you!" shouted Penny, "You don't need any excuse to get Bunion angry; she does it well enough on her own!"

"She's right; this is no good for anyone," agreed Buster as he approached the rock table.

"First, promise," said Sally. "Promise that we can come back."

Penny, not able to help herself, sat in one of the rock chairs. *It is strange,* she thought, *that we have never come upon this rock formation before.* She experienced something as she sat there, a feeling she had almost forgotten—it was a sense of wonder. And for the tiniest second, she forgot about the cold, dark halls of the Bunion Home and was simply happy.

Buster noticed something odd about these rocks, and, being analytical and scientific, he tried to puzzle out what it was. *Certainly there are rocks which are accidentally chairs and tables,* he thought, *but these stones seem— what is the word?—comfortable.* And taking a seat in one, his hunch was confirmed. Strangest of all, the surface of the rocks was perfectly smooth, as if worn from previous users. This thought sent a chill colder than the snowy air up Buster's spine.

"Yes, do promise," said Ant to Penny, hopping down from his throne.

"What, then?" said Penny, who was distracted by how lived-in the rock chair seemed.

"Promise we will come back!" Sally reminded her.

"Yes, yes, another time, but right now we must get back to the Bunion Home."

"You *promise*?" said Sally to Penny.

"I promise."

"Do you promise?" said Ant to Buster.

"Promise."

"Come on before the snow starts up again," Penny said.

And as they walked home, they looked back at the curious rock formation, afraid that, once they left it, the stone room might disappear behind the curtain of snow flurries and be forever lost among the trees heavy with frost.

CHAPTER FOUR

Secrets

I t never occurred to the fisherman and his wife that they should stand up to the rising tide of others' ignorance toward their son and his ever-growing horn. They were the puppets of small minds and were ashamed of Bucky because the small minds told them to be.

And so it was that Bucky spent most of his early days out at sea with his father, tying nets and staying out of the way. Keeping Bucky out of the way was very important to the fisherman and his wife. People talk; what would the neighbors think; we don't want to upset anyone—these were the excuses the fisherman and his wife made for hiding Bucky, and they were the walls of Bucky's prison. There was only one of him, and so many others who were afraid or put off by the sight of Bucky—the math, his parents reasoned, was not in Bucky's favor.

One day while they were fishing, Bucky lost his balance and fell horn-first into the cold, dark sea. The fisherman, who knew that Bucky had never been in the water before, quickly threw a large net out for Bucky to take hold of. Seconds passed like hours, no sign of Bucky in sight. Just as the fisherman was about to leap in after him, Bucky's horn sliced the water as his head and body shot up like a bullet.

"Bucky!" shouted the fisherman with relief.

Bucky hadn't drowned at all and was swimming as if he had been born underwater! As he splashed, he made the most wonderful sound—a sound the fisherman had never heard him make. It was the sound of laughter.

From then on, Bucky spent most of his days in the ocean while his father fished. On land, Bucky was clumsy and wary of every movement, as his horn unbalanced him and caused him to hunch over. But underwater! Underwater, he was agile and free, as if he were flying! And his horn was like a rudder, giving him control and speed he had never dreamed of. And the strange treasures of this new realm! Fish of all colors, some bigger than his father's boat and others as small as his baby toe, and none of them bothered in the least by the horn that grew from his forehead! *This is a place full of secret magic,* thought Bucky, *and—unlike the land, with its scowling and frowning people—this realm is mine alone.*

For the first time in his short life, Bucky felt normal. He almost felt—but this was nonsense, he knew—that this was where he belonged.

* * *

Out of the ocean, there were other secrets that Bucky sought to know—the secrets of numbers and words, and the pieces of the puzzle that made up the world. And after dreaming about it for as long as he could remember, the day for Bucky to begin school finally arrived.

"You'll make do, won't you?" asked his mother, giving him a look that said he wouldn't.

"Keep out of the way then," advised his father somewhat sadly.

And with that, they sent him on his way.

* * *

"Have you seen anything like it before, Professor?" said Mrs. Onion to Dr. Bloogle, the science teacher. Upon seeing Bucky seated in the classroom, and without even a word of hello, Mrs. Onion immediately had sent for a scientific analysis of this oddly deformed child.

"I certainly have not," replied Dr. Bloogle as he measured the length of Bucky's horn. "Unless you count hexagonal brain," he intoned, "and I wouldn't, not before lunch."

This sounded very scientific indeed to Mrs. Onion. And while she had no idea what he was saying, it was certainly not her place to doubt the doctor. "Of course, of course," she replied, "and what do you think the… prognostication is for learning and retention, Doctor?"

"Hmm…" pondered Dr. Bloogle, his fingers in Bucky's ears. "I would say the specimen, because of the *probiquitous* malformation escalating from the *lobal flange,* is, therefore, *sub-cortexual* and—this is before lunch?—therefore *incapacitable* to squirming and prevention."

"Yes, I see," said Mrs. Onion, not at all seeing, but not wanting to appear out of touch with current scientific data. "So your recommendation, then, would be...no?"

"Yes, no. Possibly modified," concluded the doctor, removing his fingers from Bucky's ears. "Now, if you will excuse me, lunch awaits."

"Well, you heard the doctor, Lucky," said Mrs. Onion to Bucky. "I'm afraid your brain malformation prohibits you from reaping the benefits of schooling."

Bucky's heart broke.

"And furthermore," continued Mrs. Onion, "your grotesque appearance would upset the other children. There are so many more of *them*...well, Lucky, the math is simply not in your favor, you see."

Bucky didn't know how to answer this, so he turned to leave.

"Perhaps," called Mrs. Onion as he sulkily ambled out, "you might enjoy fishing?"

* * *

Bucky went to a cliff overlooking the ocean and cried his own sea of tears. He wanted only a way to belong. Yet the more he looked for goodness in others, the less he found it, and the less he wanted to belong.

Far down below, he watched a fisherman pulling empty nets into his boat—a dot on the vast blue horizon.

It was the last time that Bucky would see his father in this world.

CHAPTER FIVE

The Graveyard of Forgotten Things

Behind a locked door and up a crooked staircase, the attic of the Bunion Home housed years of clutter draped in cobwebs. None of the extra children had ever been up these stairs and past this door, for Miss Bunion had the only key. Aside from Miss Bunion herself, no current residents—not even Ursa the cook—had seen its hidden corners. There were stories that the attic housed Miss Bunion's army of bats that stole the souls of children in their sleep. Some whispered that two witches—Miss Bunion's sisters—lived in the attic, and each night she joined them at their cauldron to brew nightmares that seeped through the walls and into their dreams.

The truth was not so bleak—the attic was merely a graveyard of forgotten things. In one corner sat a large wooden trunk, its heavy brass hasp and hinges rusted and tarnished. And it was no wonder why Miss Bunion never opened it, since it contained evidence of a terrible secret—a secret she intended to take to her grave.

On top of the trunk sat a crystal ball on a thick marble base. The inside of the ball was carpeted with white crystals, on top of which sat a miniature carousel circled by six horses, two lions, an ostrich, and a buffalo. Though they appeared frozen in the glass, the carousel animals turned when the key under the base was wound, and the white crystals stirred slowly around them as the strangest music played.

But it had been a very long time since the globe's curious song had played and the carousel had turned, for Miss Bunion kept it covered with an old black curtain. For years, the snow globe had sat here—dormant with unused magic, its animals never moving—and now it merely kept shut the trunk that housed the clues to the dark secret buried deep in Miss Bunion's stone heart.

Leaning on one side of the trunk, laced in a cocoon of cobwebs, sat a heavy scroll, its edges curled and yellowed with age. If we had been able to sneak up the creaking stairs and into this graveyard of forgotten things, and if we had pulled the cobwebs from this heavy scroll and unfurled it, we would have seen that it was a canvas on which was painted a detailed and fantastic map. Exotic creatures leaped from a roiling sea at the edge of a great island, and hovering over this—seeming to float above the territory—the paths of stars and planets were traced with fine paint strokes.

Whoever had painted this strange map was an artist of great skill, for it filled the eyes and danced in the mind of anyone who saw it. But here it stayed—hidden, collecting dust—as it, too, was part of Miss Bunion's awful secret. The canvas had been roughly cut, as if torn from its frame, and was fraying and ripped in places. Though it was filled with strange symbols and names, the artist had not signed the canvas. Only its title, painted in a swirling, elegant cursive and centered neatly at the top, gave a clue to its meaning and history; "The Place of No Place," it read.

Still, if Miss Bunion hated these things and wanted to keep their secrets forever, why not destroy them? Why keep the globe and the map, and the trunk full of terrible memories? Surely, she did not expect to need them again.

* * *

Having finished their breakfast of bark patties and radish juice, the children went off to their morning chores. As Ant, Sally, Penny, and Buster were out gathering twigs and leaves for Ursa to stew for their dinner, they headed far into the woods to find the stone room again.

"I see it!" cried Sally after they had walked nearly a mile.

"There it is," said Ant. "The snow has melted, and now it's even more of a room than before."

They ran to the now-uncovered rock formation. Ant and Buster sat at the table while Penny and Sally headed to the large chairs.

"There is something funny about this," Buster theorized, "but I can't quite put my finger on it."

"It's magic; that's what it is," replied Ant.

"To a scientist, there is no such thing as magic," said Buster.

"I think it is part of a castle which is buried deep in the earth; only this part is sticking up," said Sally.

"They're smooth and shiny, but only on top," said Penny, "like they've been used...*lived* in, almost."

"It's only water—water and ice which have worn the rock smooth," said Buster. "Very simple, really." Buster was the only one of them who could read—learning was not a priority for extra children at the Bunion Home. But he was very curious, and Ursa taught him in secret lessons with books she smuggled in from the town library.

"Water?" asked Ant. "But the river is miles from here. Where did the water come from, and why wouldn't *all* the rocks be smooth?"

Buster was unaccustomed to critical inquiry, and didn't know what to say. "Well...there must be some reason," he began. "That's how science works, after all." But his faith in science was beginning to waver.

"I *feel* something here," said Sally, coming down from her rock throne. "Do you feel it too?"

"It feels strange," said Penny.

"Sort of…dead," replied Ant.

"Well, something's missing," said Buster. "An explanation—"

"The story," said Sally. "The story of this place is what's missing!"

Like all children, the extra children of the Bunion Home longed for stories. But, unlike other children, they had no stories of their own, as they had no parents to tell them theirs nor any memories of their lives before arriving at the Bunion Home.

"Well, maybe we should look for the story," said Penny.

Buster laughed. "Penny, you can't *look* for a story; you can only look for facts," he said. "That's just basic science."

"Well, what do you call this, then?" said Sally as she crawled from under one of the stone tables. In her hands, she held four pieces of wood, each decorated with ornate carvings that shimmered with hints of gold. At the edges, each piece came to a sharp angle.

"What did you find, Sally?" asked Ant. "Is it the story?"

"Where did this come from?" asked Penny.

"Under here," said Sally, bending under the table, "in a shelf hidden under the rock."

Buster laid the wood on the stone table for a better look. On the back of each piece, he saw written words and noticed that some edges were beveled, while others were slotted, as if they might fit together like puzzle pieces.

"I found it. I found the story!" cried Sally. "At least the first part."

"Maybe you have, Sally," said Buster, becoming more curious each minute. "Maybe you have."

Miss Bunion was not in her graveyard of forgotten things at the moment little Sally made her discovery under the stone table deep in that cold forest. Had she been there, Miss Bunion might have heard the faintest strains of music seeping from under the heavy cloth that cloaked the glass snow globe. And had she lifted the dusty black curtain which hid it, Miss Bunion would have seen the carousel within the globe make one slow full turn, as if under a spell, stirring up little clouds of snow as it circled.

CHAPTER SIX

Rare and Astounding
Wonderments of Nature

As Bucky sat on the rock by the cliff, more alone than any other creature on land or sea, he cried so many tears that they formed a pool at his feet. He looked down at the tears filling the dark earth where he stood, and for the first time saw his own reflection. He marveled at the long, spiraling horn which so offended all the people in his village—they said it was the work of demons, or made him stupid—and realized it only made him different. And it was merely this difference that the townsfolk hated so.

For the first time, Bucky looked at his horn in close detail. He held his breath at the sight—it was the most amazing thing he had ever seen. It shone with every color imaginable—deep blue and shimmering violet amid swirls of gleaming white and translucent gray. It reminded him of the oyster shells and black pearls that were sold at the market. How was it that he had never truly *seen* it before? And why did no one else see what he saw? *How wrong they are,* he thought. *The math may not be in my favor, but* magnificence *is!*

And for the first time Bucky didn't care what the world thought of him. Like the grain of sand that becomes the oyster's pearl, Bucky was but an irritant to his surroundings. Yet he knew that, like the pearl, he too was a thing of rare brilliance.

* * *

"Don't move—stay just as you are!" the man's voice boomed.

Bucky froze.

"I want to record every detail of this historic and momentous occasion in the vast library of my brain, just as I'm witnessing it before me!"

Bucky stayed still. "Who...who are you, and what do you want?" he said anxiously. "I'm not a demon, and I'm not stupid. Understand?"

"Of course! Of course, you're not, good sir!" replied the voice, "Of that I have no doubt in the slightest! Now, kindly turn around, if you please."

Bucky turned and found himself facing a most peculiar man—tall and thin, with a thick black mustache that looped back in on itself. He wore a long red coat, a tall black hat, and white gloves.

"Most impressive!" said the man, mesmerized by Bucky's horn. "Most impressive indeed!"

"Thank you, I suppose," began Bucky. "You aren't afraid of catching demons?"

"Quite the opposite, quite the opposite, good sir!" the man continued. "Why, don't you know that I am a discoverer and presenter of rare and astounding wonderments of nature?"

"I didn't know," answered Bucky. "I'm just Bucky."

"Bucky!" cried the man, grabbing Bucky's hand in his own and shaking it vigorously. "A fine name for a fine creature. Yes, yes! A pleasure to make your acquaintance!"

"Thank you, I suppose, Mr…"

"Cornelius Granville Barker, Esquire, at your service!"

"Pleased to meet you, Mr. Barker." Bucky's head was spinning—usually, when he met the eyes of another person, he saw only sad pity or fear. But this man's eyes glistened with fascination.

"Such a marvelously unusual attribute the likes of which I've never seen," said Mr. Barker, still mesmerized by Bucky's horn. "Please tell me, young man… what is your current status of employ?"

Bucky was confused. "I…I don't understand."

"Yes, yes, forgive me. I mean to say, what is it that you *do* Monsieur Bucky?"

Bucky thought about this a bit. "Well…I wanted more than anything to attend school, so I could read the books in the library. But the teachers think my horn makes me stupid, and they turned me away."

"Most unfortunate, most unfortunate!" said Barker, shaking his head.

"I go fishing with my father," Bucky continued, "but mostly I just…stay out of the way."

"Out of the way?" cried Cornelius Barker. "Why, that is certainly no place for such a unique being as yourself!"

"The math is not in my favor, you see," explained Bucky. "There are so many of *them*, and only one of me."

"Them?"

"People who are, well…normal. Who don't stick out."

Cornelius Barker let out a hearty laugh. "Why, of course the math is not in your favor—*magnificence* is, dear boy, magnificence is!"

A chill went up Bucky's spine, and he broke out in laughter as well. "Do you really think so?"

"My dear Bucky—I don't *think*, I *know*…and remember: I am an expert in such matters!" Mr. Barker pulled from his sleeve a white card, which Bucky saw was filled with fancy script. "Allow me to read the inscription for your benefit, good sir." Mr. Barker held the elegantly engraved card carefully at the edges, following the words with a white-gloved finger as he read aloud, "Cornelius Barker's Traveling Exhibition of Rare and Astounding Wonderments of Nature, and Flea Circus. Cornelius Granville Barker, Master of Ceremonies."

Bucky's eyes widened, and his head swam with possibilities. "Is that…what you suppose I am—a…*wonderment* of nature?"

"My good sir, I've never laid eyes on a more wonderful wonderment in all my years!" exclaimed Mr. Barker. "Come, let me show you."

He led Bucky down a winding path to a carriage. Hitched to the carriage were four miniature ponies, which were much like any other ponies, except that they were fiery orange with deep-blue manes. On the side of the carriage, the words "BARKER'S RARE AND ASTOUNDING WONDERMENTS OF NATURE, AND FLEA CIRCUS" were written in swirling gold script.

Barker opened the carriage door. "After you, good sir."

"I don't know if I should. It's almost dinnertime, and I should get back to town."

"The town?" Cornelius laughed. "But, my dear Bucky, I offer the world! It doesn't hurt to take a look."

Bucky thought of the faces of the townsfolk, their scowls and scorn, and pointing fingers. "I suppose it doesn't," he said, getting in the carriage.

They followed a winding path down from the high cliff, to a field just outside of town. The field was dotted with a patchwork of multicolored tents and large painted banners. Barker led Bucky inside a large blue-and white-striped tent.

"Mr. Big," said Mr. Barker to a very large man who was shaped like a balloon.

Mr. Big sighed. With a large magnifying glass, he was peering into a small box. "The fleas are having trouble with the teeter-totter," he said in a high, squeaky voice that surprised Bucky. "The trapeze is coming along nicely, however."

"Very good, very good," answered Barker. "Big, I'd like you to meet the newest addition to our...menagerie."

"Now, Barker, how do you expect me to rehearse the tightrope—" Here, his voice broke off, for he had turned around to face what seemed to be a boy with a horn growing straight out of his forehead. "Yow-ee!" he exclaimed, because that is what he said when he was surprised.

"As you see, Mr. Bucky has been blessed with a unique gift," replied Mr. Barker.

"Indeed, indeed!" said Mr. Big, fascinated by the spiraling horn that seemed to change colors depending on how the light hit it. "Ever so pleased to make your acquaintance, Mr. Bucky." He shook Bucky's hand, which was swallowed by Mr. Big's enormous fingers.

"Mr. Big is an expert in the field of flea wrangling...as well as one of our star attractions," explained Mr. Barker. "You see, dear Bucky, we are in the business of traveling entertainments, and the flea circus is one of our most popular acts."

"I've never seen anything like it," marveled Bucky as he squinted to see the tiny fleas in the box. Some were dressed as clowns, and others rode tiny bicycles.

"Indeed, you haven't," squeaked Mr. Big, "as it is the world's first." In addition to flea wrangling, Mr. Big's main talent was singing opera arias in his high voice while accompanying himself on the musical saw.

"Come…meet some more of your new family," said Mr. Barker as he parted the canvas of the tent's exit.

Barker led Bucky to the large red-and-white tent across the field, where the human performers of Barker's Traveling Exhibition of Rare and Astounding Wonderments of Nature were practicing their arts. And what wonderments they were! Bucky met Fire Man, who conjured a dancing flame in the palm of his hand, tossed it into the air, and caught it in his mouth. Contortia twisted her nimble body into undreamed-of shapes and winked at Bucky while scratching her left ear with the tip of her right toe. Mr. Backwards spoke only in reverse, which made conversation difficult, and Madame Lizardo— who had scales instead of skin and could walk up walls— welcomed him with a cup of hyacinth tea.

Here were so many others not like him, but also not like anyone else either—the math was in nobody's favor. Bucky complimented them all on their unique abilities and thanked Mr. Barker for introducing him.

"Mr. Barker," Bucky began, "I'm sorry I don't have a talent of my own."

"Don't be silly—of course, you do!"

"I can tie fishing nets, and I'm a good swimmer… but no one cares about that."

Barker raised his eyebrows in surprise. "You have no idea, do you, young man?"

"About what?"

"Why, of who you *are*," said Barker. "Or *what* you are."

Bucky's spine tingled. In all of Bucky's encounters with others, no one had bothered to tell him who or what he was, except to call him a demon or freak. "Mr. Barker…do *you* know what I am?"

Barker leaned down and whispered as if sharing a deep secret, "Why, my good sir, you are the *Narwhal Boy* himself!"

Bucky was speechless, mesmerized by the reflection of his horn in Barker's wide, dark eyes. "Let me educate you," Barker said.

In his personal tent, Barker reached for a thick book whose cover was made of wood. It reminded Bucky of the days he had spent in the town library. "You've heard of unicorns, I presume?" asked Barker as he turned the musty pages in a fog of dust.

Bucky hadn't, but he nodded just the same.

Barker landed on a page. "*Monodon monoceros*," he said, pointing to a large mass suspended in blue light.

Bucky's eyes lit up. "I know this!" he cried. "In the library, I saw it in a book… I think it's called a whale."

"Not just any whale," replied Barker, "but the narwhal—the most majestic and regal creature ever to swim the ocean!"

"Nar-whal," said Bucky, trying out the word. He ran his finger over the picture, as if to touch the creature's spiraling horn and mottled gray skin. Bucky brought his fingers to his own forehead, tracing the mutation that protruded from it. "Narwhal," he said again, thinking that finally he had found himself.

And so it was, through Cornelius Barker and his Astounding Wonderments of Nature, that the pearl born to the fisherman and his wife escaped the indifferent oyster of his former world. He was no longer just Bucky—for now and evermore, he was Bucky the Narwhal Boy.

CHAPTER SEVEN

The Frame
with No Picture

"They fit together at the edges," said Buster as the others watched on with wonder. They were so excited at seeing Sally's discovery that they hardly noticed it was nearly dinnertime. But the Stone Room and its mysteries were irresistible. To all but Penny, it seemed.

"We need to get back at once," she said firmly, "before we catch cold and miss dinner."

"This is more important," said Buster as he wedged the last corner to complete the wooden rectangle. "It's some kind of frame—"

"Bunion will have our heads!" said Penny. "Now, let's all be sensible!"

"Please, let's not," begged Sally. "I hate stewed leaves, and this is much more fun."

"Go if you like," said Buster. "I, for one, am staying."

"Me too," said Ant.

"Me too," said Sally.

Penny gave Buster an angry look. "Fine, we all stay," she said as the sky began to darken.

It was a sight to behold—detailed carving with flecks of gold deep in the grooves that lined the perimeter of the frame. The children had never seen an ocean, but if they had, they might say these engravings resembled the rough waves of a stormy sea.

"All right, so it's a frame," said Penny, rejoining them.

"Only there's no picture for it," noted Ant.

"Look," said Sally, pointing to a bit of stiff material on one side of the frame. "The picture's been torn out."

"She's right; there *was* a picture...but it's gone now," said Penny, becoming more curious.

"The writing, what does it say?" asked Ant. They had been so entranced by the elegant frame that they nearly forgot what was on the back.

"Read it, Buster, so we can be done and go home," said Penny.

He picked up the frame and stared intently at its back. On each of the four sides was written a phrase, so Buster had to turn the frame completely around to read them all.

"The picture is no picture..." he began slowly, "but the place of No Place...a wish opens the world... and the mirror has no face."

For a moment, there was silence, as no one knew what to say. Buster laid the frame back down on the stone table.

"A wish," said Sally finally, and without even knowing it, she made one.

"A wish opens the world," said Ant, and thinking it, he made one too.

"We should all get back," said Penny. "We're in trouble as it is."

But no one heard because they were all staring at the picture with no picture, and they were frozen by what they saw. For at that moment, the part of the stone table within the square of the picture frame began to move. It swirled and rippled as if suddenly liquid. Fog crept out of the frame's edges as the rippling surface seemed to fall away into nothingness, leaving a gray void.

"Do you see what I'm seeing?" said Buster, not moving an inch.

"What just happened?" asked Penny.

"Listen...I hear water," said Ant.

"Birds too," said Sally.

And before the others realized it, Sally had climbed atop the stone table and was peering down into the frame. For an instant, there was only the sound of her small scream as she fell through the picture with no picture.

Ant was the one who noticed Sally's fingers clinging to the wood, and without thinking, he ran to grab her arm. But he was not strong enough, and the rock was slick with ice.

In the blink of an eye, they were both gone.

"Ant!" shrieked Penny.

"Sally!" shouted Buster as he and Penny scrambled onto the table.

"What do we do?" cried Penny.

"We have no choice… Come on!" yelled Buster. He grabbed Penny's arm and leaped in.

As they began to fall, Buster snatched a corner of the wooden rectangle, thinking that they might need it to get back from wherever they were going.

And so the frame with no picture followed them, leaving only the stone table, dusted with snow, jutting from the cold, silent earth.

CHAPTER EIGHT

Bucky the Narwhal Boy

"Step right up! Step right up! See the strange marriage of land and sea before your very own eyes!" Cornelius Barker was a born showman. "In the flesh…Bucky the Narwhal Boy, Prince of the Sea!"

It had been three years since Bucky joined Barker's menagerie of exceptional wonders, and though Bucky couldn't say he was unhappy, he couldn't say he was happy either. He had thought traveling would bring experience and knowledge, but so far it had brought only the dreary boredom of routine. Day in and day out, he spent hours in his tank, swimming for the benefit of gawking strangers. He speared rings with his horn to display his aquatic dexterity, or jumped high out of the water, splashing the onlookers. He was an astounding swimmer, sometimes staying underwater for minutes at a time without coming up for air. Over his tank was hung a colorful banner depicting, from Barker's book, the horned whale amid the swirling deep of the ocean. The words "THE AMAZING NARWHAL BOY" were splashed across it in large red letters.

Once, Bucky had thought himself magnificent. But, here, he did not feel magnificent or even exceptional. What he felt was ordinary—very ordinary. There was no honor in what he did, and he knew that those who paid to gape and stare at him in his tank saw what they wanted to see and not really what was there. He began to realize that, whatever Bucky the Narwhal Boy was, it was not really Bucky. Mostly, it was a *thing*—a curiosity, a story to pass on. And like any story, it depended not on him for its value, but rather on the person telling the story. In this way, Bucky was reduced, in the minds of those who saw him, to his one exceptional trait. No one walked away thinking, *There is a young man with dreams*, or *That one has a sharp mind and noble spirit*. No, the one and only thought the world gave Bucky was, *Look— there's a horn growing out of that boy's forehead!* And this made Bucky sad.

One day, Barker's Traveling Exhibition of Rare and Astounding Wonderments of Nature, and Flea Circus pitched their tents near a carnival by the sea. Bucky spent hours gazing out at the ocean, remembering his days swimming from his father's fishing boat. He had been, he decided, truly magnificent then, swimming free in the boundless waters teeming with exotic life.

Through the side of his tank, Bucky saw a strange contraption being assembled—a round base circled by vertical poles, and on each pole was a colorfully painted animal. He counted six horses, two lions, an ostrich, and a buffalo. After it was all set up, the animals began to move around the center pole, as if chasing one another's tails in an endless, circling race. And music began to play— a strange and soothing melody. He thought he had seen something similar in the flea circus, but he never dreamed he'd see such a thing that was human-sized.

"Barker! Mr. Barker!" whispered Bucky over the edge of his tank.

"Yes, a break…in due time, kind sir," replied Barker. "And do keep your voice down—a Narwhal Boy, being primitive and sea-dwelling, does not speak our language, as you know."

"No, that's not it," said Bucky, lowering his voice and thinking himself neither primitive nor sea-dwelling. "I want to know what that is." He pointed with his horn to the strange contraption behind him.

"That? Of course, that is a merry-go-round."

Bucky stared blankly.

"A *carousel*," Barker explained, "an amusement for children, you see."

Bucky watched it turn and noticed each animal wore a saddle. "Can I?" pleaded Bucky.

"Can you what?"

"Can I ride it? I am still a boy, after all."

Barker's laugh stung Bucky. "But of course you cannot. I'm sorry, good sir."

"But why not?" Bucky asked.

Barker sighed deeply. "My dear Bucky," he began, "don't you see? You are special—a rare and astounding wonderment of nature indeed. And how would it look for our Narwhal Boy to leave his tank, and walk and talk like all the other children?"

"But I *am* like all the other children…in most ways," Bucky offered.

"In all ways except one," said Barker.

"In all ways that matter," said Bucky.

"Bucky, Bucky, Bucky," began Barker, shaking his head, "do you know what you are to them? Do you know what would happen if you left this tank and walked over to that carousel? I'll tell you what. They'd fear you. They'd make fun of you, shun you, and yes…even hate you. And why? Because of this." Barker tugged on Bucky's horn. "But here, in your tank"—Barker's tone changed from buzzing bee to honey—"under this banner, you are magical, an exotic star shining under this unclouded sky. Out there, among them, they will give you only their scorn. But in your tank, you are Bucky the Narwhal Boy, Prince of the Sea."

Bucky's heart sank.

"And those who would look on you with disdain in *their* world regard you here with wonder, and hold their breath in awe."

Bucky was silent as he considered Barker's words. He was sad, too, for he realized that Barker wasn't much different from all the others he had encountered on land. After a moment that seemed to last forever, Bucky mustered the courage to speak. "Mr. Barker, I want to please ride the carousel," he said. "Bucky the *person* would like to ride the carousel."

Mr. Barker's eyebrows went up in surprise at Bucky's willfulness, and he let out a wicked laugh. "My dear sir," he said, the bees returning to his voice, "I don't know who that is."

* * *

"Hortense, I want the white horse," said a young girl as she stepped onto the carousel.

"Well...I want the white horse too, Isabella," Hortense replied.

Isabella smiled sadly, used to her sister being difficult. "Very well, I'll take the ostrich then."

Hortense, suspicious, changed her mind. "Well... *I* want the ostrich." Before Isabella could respond, Hortense shoved her ticket into the operator's hand and jumped aboard the ostrich.

Isabella laughed to herself. *Hortense always seems to see the dark clouds and never the rainbows,* she thought, *and is often unpleasant for no reason at all.* Isabella gave the man her ticket and climbed onto the white horse.

Hortense turned around and stuck her tongue out at her sister.

As the music began to play, the animals trotted in their slow circle. During the ride, Isabella laughed and carried on with the other children, but Hortense just frowned at her sister. As the carousel turned, Isabella saw the most peculiar sight on each rotation—a boy, about her own age, floating in a large tank of water, staring at them with sad eyes. And there was something strange about him, something on his head that she couldn't quite make out.

"I'm telling father," said Hortense as they left the carousel.

"Telling him what?" asked Isabella, who was walking toward the tank with the strange boy in it.

"I'm telling him you tried to trick me. You wanted me to ride the white horse, but I knew better."

"Oh, do as you please," said Isabella, who was tired of her sister's bickering. "It makes no difference to me."

"We'll see about that," fumed Hortense, storming off.

* * *

Bucky floated in his tank with a sad heart and wondered who he was. He realized that, even as a rare and astounding wonderment of nature, he was still all alone in the world. To cheer himself up, he watched the carousel and the bright faces of the boys and girls as they rode it. He watched the most beautiful girl get on the white horse. Another girl was teasing her, but it didn't seem to matter—the girl on the white horse seemed unclouded by hate or ill will. Bucky wished he could say hello to the girl on the white horse, to see her up close and know her name. And as he wished this, his sadness lifted, and he was full of hope.

The carousel stopped and Bucky's heart skipped a beat, for the girl got off the white horse and was walking towards him.

"Does it hurt?" said the girl from the white horse to Bucky.

He peeked over the edge of the glass, not wanting to frighten her. "Excuse me," he said, as if to apologize for existing at all.

"The thing on your head," the girl explained, "does it hurt?"

Bucky smiled and pulled himself up farther. "No, not anymore," he replied. In spite of himself, he laughed.

"Why are you laughing?"

"Because no one has ever asked me that before."

"Really? Not even your mother and father?"

Bucky couldn't stop staring at her. "No, not even my mother and father."

"Well, I'm glad anyway."

"Glad?"

"That it doesn't hurt, silly," she said, and they both laughed. "My name is Isabella."

"My name is Bucky."

"May I touch it?"

"You're not afraid?"

"What's to be afraid of?"

"Nothing, I suppose," said Bucky, giggling. "Nothing at all." And he lowered his head so she could touch his horn.

"It's wonderful."

Bucky turned away because, though he didn't understand why, he thought he might cry.

"What's wrong?"

"I don't know," said Bucky. "You're just so...kind, and I don't know why."

Isabella laughed. "You're silly. I like you."

"Well, I like you too." And for that moment he didn't feel so alone.

The girl who was teasing Isabella and a man approached them, and the spell was broken.

"Here she is, Father," grumbled the girl who had ridden the ostrich. "She tricked me, just as I said."

"Enough, Hortense, life is too short for tattling," said the man.

"Father, Hortense, I'd like you to meet Bucky," said Isabella.

"Well, hello, young man," said the father, trying to hide his surprise at the appendage growing out of the boy's forehead.

"Ick! It's disgusting!" said Hortense. "Father, tell Isabella to leave it at once!"

Bucky lowered himself back into the tank.

"Hortense, why are you so mean?" said Isabella. "Don't listen to her, Bucky; you're magnificent. Isn't he, father?"

"Well, yes…certainly remarkable," said the father politely.

"It's awful, and I refuse to stand here looking at it," said Hortense.

"Hortense, where are your manners?" chided the father. "However, it is getting late, and we should be on our way."

Bucky gazed intently at Isabella, as if to record her smiling face in his memory.

"Goodbye, Bucky," said Isabella. "It was a pleasure to make your acquaintance." She reached her hand up towards him.

Bucky reached down and their fingers touched. "Goodbye," Bucky said as he watched the girl who rode the white horse stroll past the carousel, its circling animals casting shadows in her path.

CHAPTER NINE

The Frigid Shore

It seemed they would never stop falling. Time slowed, and their descent was like a dream of flight. But then the four bodies sliced through a heavy fog and splashed down into the coldest water.

"Help!" cried Sally.

"I can't swim!" yelled Ant.

But, somehow, they were swimming, all of them. Later, they would wonder if the mysterious creature who roamed these waters helped them to safety, but at this moment, survival was the only thought in their minds.

Buster was the first to pull himself to shore, and he helped the others onto the hard-packed sand.

"Where are we?" said Sally through shivers.

"I think we're at the edge of the world," said Buster, who had never been more than a mile from the Bunion Home—much less seen a lake or ocean before.

"I'm freezing!" cried Ant.

"Maybe we're dead," said Penny.

"Don't be so gloomy, Penny. We're not dead," said Buster.

"How can you tell?" asked Sally.

Buster was silent.

"Well, come on then, smarty face," snapped Penny.

Buster was annoyed at this. "We can't be dead," he began, "because dead people can't swim."

This seemed to satisfy everyone for the moment.

"Well, we still don't know where we are," said Penny.

And from behind them on the beach, a deep voice boomed, "No Place."

They all turned at once, and were surprised to see a large animal lazily chewing seagrass. Its coat was white as snow, which made it all the more startling.

"Who said that?" called Buster, glancing around to find the person who had spoken.

"Eek!" cried Penny, who was easily frightened.

"Excuse me, but you are very big for a dog," said Sally, not at all afraid of the huge beast.

"Come out, whoever you are!" shouted Buster, still looking for the owner of the voice.

"It's not a dog, silly," said Ant. "It's a *horse*, and be careful you don't make it mad."

The creature raised its head slowly and looked at each of them. "I am neither, thank you just the same," the animal said in his deep, slow voice. He lowered his head back to the seagrass.

"You talk!" cried Sally. "I've never seen a talking animal before."

"Well, I've never had anyone to talk to before," he said.

"You're the color of snow," said Sally.

"If you're not a dog, and not a horse, what are you?" asked Penny.

He raised his head and swept it slowly from side to side, meeting their eyes. "I am a buffalo, though I have not always been." His eyes were heavy with sorrow.

"We don't know where we are," said Ant. "Do you?"

"As I said before—No Place," answered the white buffalo.

"Well what does that mean?" asked Buster.

The buffalo inclined his head toward Buster. "I believe you brought the answer to that question with you," he said, gesturing with his large black nose.

In all the confusion, Buster had forgotten that he'd reached for the picture frame before their fall. It had washed up on the beach, just a few yards away. Buster picked up the frame and read the words on the back again, "The picture is no picture…but the place of No Place…" He asked, "This is a place called…No Place?"

"No Place, yes," said the buffalo.

"Everyone, look!" cried Ant, pointing to a spot far down the beach.

"What is that?" cried Sally, squinting to see.

The white buffalo slowly turned his head and looked down the shore with sad eyes. "That," he said with a heavy sigh, "is the wreckage of abandoned dreams."

* * *

As a thing, it was, in its way, more unsettling to the children than the sight of a talking buffalo. All four ran to investigate, the slow animal lumbering along behind them.

Grand in size, with most of its canopied roof ripped away by the wind, it stood cockeyed and half-buried in the sand. Only a handful of wooden animals remained, their paint chipped and faded, forever stuck to their rusting poles.

"How awful!" said Sally.

"It's a carousel," said Buster. "Ursa showed me one in a book."

"But it's ruined now," said Penny.

Ant pulled some seaweed from one of the bottom gears. "How did it get here?" he asked the white buffalo.

"You will know the story soon," the white buffalo replied. "Eventually, it will be taken by the sea. Then nothing will be left."

"I don't understand," said Buster, who traced a wooden lion's roaring mouth with his fingers.

"I wish we could ride it," said Sally. "I wish it were new and not broken."

"Save your wishes, little girl," said the buffalo. "They will do you no good here."

Sally was cold and hungry. Seeing the ruined carousel and hearing the words of the white buffalo made her cry.

"Listen, mister…buffalo," said Penny sternly, "what do you mean making a little girl cry like that?"

The white buffalo sighed, and his lids hung heavily on his brown eyes. "I mean to say there's no hope left," he said, turning to Sally. "I'm sorry you're sad." He nudged Sally with his cold nose, then narrowed his large eyes and looked to the sky. "The sun is low; he will be here soon. We must leave him to his work."

"Who?" asked Buster.

The white buffalo stared out to the sea. "Follow me; you can watch from behind the seagrass."

Crouching in the dunes, the children waited with the white buffalo. A few minutes later, just as the sun was lowering into the sea, a strange creature emerged from the surf and clambered onto the beach in front of the carousel. A tangle of seaweed and shells covered its body, obscuring its shape. As the creature stood and walked to the ruined carousel, the orphans saw that the creature was a man.

The man from the sea moved as if in a trance, carefully removing the shells and kelp from each carousel animal. When he was done, he kissed one of the horses on the nose before calmly walking back into the sea.

"He's sad too," said Sally.

"Who was that?" asked Buster.

The white buffalo sighed. "Come. Climb on my back." He knelt on his front legs. "You need to get warm, and there's much to tell you."

With the four orphans in tow, the white buffalo ambled down a well-worn path through the seagrass and into the woods beyond.

* * *

Back in the great dining hall of the Bunion Home, the other children sat on the long benches, preparing to eat their dinner of twig-and-leaf chowder. Miss Bunion surveyed the room and noticed four bowls sitting in front of an empty bench. "Ursa," she called to the rotund cook, "what is wrong with tonight's dinner?"

Ursa was dragging her vat of chowder back to the kitchen. She stopped in her tracks and took a taste from her ladle. "Not enough salt?" she answered.

"There are *four empty chairs* in this dining room."

"Ah, so there are."

"WELL?" snapped Miss Bunion, causing Ursa to drop her ladle.

"Y-Yes, ma'am?" she timidly replied.

"WHERE ARE THEY?" Miss Bunion shrieked as Ursa leaped back in fright, causing the vat to crash to the floor.

"They were gathering leaves in the woods, Miss Bunion, ma'am." Ursa's voice quaked, as she feared Miss Bunion's wrath as much as the extra children did.

"WELL GO FIND THEM!" thundered Miss Bunion.

The room of children froze with fear.

"And as for the rest of you *miserable urchins*," she hissed, "there will be no supper tonight. Now, go to bed at once!" Miss Bunion stormed out of the dining hall, the heavy door rattling as it slammed behind her.

As the children rushed out of the dining hall and to their bunk beds, Miss Bunion headed to the attic. Whether it was something far back in her memory which sent her there, or simply her anger at the empty dining chairs, we cannot be certain. Creaking up the crooked stairs to her graveyard of forgotten things, Miss Bunion's small and dark heart skipped a beat as she heard a sound coming from behind the attic's door. It was a sound she had not heard in decades—the strange music from the carousel in the glass dome.

Her crooked hands trembled with rage as she turned the key in the lock. The four wicked children had somehow snuck into her private fortress—she was certain of it. But the attic was empty, save for the forgotten things that lay dormant among the cobwebs. With disbelieving ears, she walked to the trunk and yanked the black curtain from the carousel dome. Inside the glass, the carousel was spinning wildly behind a flurry of snow. *This is impossible*, she knew, but as she thought this, the scrolled canvas leaning on the trunk's side began fluttering as if to spite her.

As she got over her shock, the meaning of what Miss Bunion was witnessing became clear to her. With thin, bony fingers, she brought the glass dome to her wrinkled face. A liquid fog—black and churning—swirled inside the glass, swallowing the carousel. Miss Bunion's dark eyes bulged, and her mouth twisted into a sinister smile.

The murky cloud inside the dome lifted. And what Miss Bunion saw inside the dome was not the swirling carousel wrapped in snow, but rather the milky vision of a ruined carousel engulfed in sand, surrounded by four children and a white buffalo.

Miss Bunion did not waste time by indulging her fury. Instead, she removed a key from the bottom of the dome and placed the snow globe on a shelf. Turning the key in the rusted lock, she freed the tarnished brass hasp of the old trunk, which had been shut tight for more years than even she could count.

CHAPTER TEN

Malice and Intrigue

As the days passed at the seaside carnival, Bucky watched the turning carousel, hoping to see his friend, Isabella, riding the white horse. But she never returned, and for the second time in his short life, Bucky felt utterly alone. He thought Mr. Barker's traveling show would allow him to live in the world, but it only drew him further away from his dream of finding a purpose.

Before, his prison was the scorn and fear of others who saw only his deformity. Now, it was the glass tank under the canvas banner that read, "THE AMAZING NARWHAL BOY." He thought he knew himself, and believed he truly *was* a narwhal boy. And for a time, he believed this meant something. But Bucky realized now that the bright-red letters above his tank said nothing about who he really was.

At night, Bucky floated in his tank and dreamed of escape as he shut his eyes tightly and wished his horn would disappear. Both seemed impossible. Mr. Barker, angered at Bucky's ingratitude and now suspicious of him, had locked a heavy iron grate over the top of Bucky's tank. Bucky was too valuable a "wonderment of nature" to lose.

And Bucky dreamed of Isabella, who had shown him kindness and had seen that there was more to him than the horn growing out of his head. In his dream, she was back on the white horse, laughing and waving to him as she circled by. And the Bucky in his dream leaped out of his tank to join her, though with each step he took toward the carousel, the farther it faded into the distance.

* * *

Hortense made sure her sister was occupied. As she expected, Isabella was sitting in the library, fiddling with the dome her father had given her as a souvenir from the carnival. Isabella was naming the carousel animals inside, who turned amid flurries of snow.

Hortense was jealous of Isabella—she was always going around being *happy,* and this infuriated Hortense. And she felt her father loved Isabella more, especially in the year that had passed since their mother died. Of course, he loved them both, but Hortense was so blinded with envy that she never noticed.

With Isabella busy in the library, Hortense tip-toed up the stairs to the attic.

"Guess what?" sneered Hortense to her cousin Grundy. Grundy Bunion and Pig Sneed were playing hide-and-destroy in the attic of the large Bunion house. It was a game of their own invention that always ended badly.

The lid of an old trunk opened, and out popped Pig. "Go eat worms!" he said to Hortense, for Pig was as polite as he was smart.

Grundy and Pig were the meanest boys Hortense knew, which is why she needed their help. "I have a secret," she said.

"Yeah? Well, tell it to the worms!" said Pig. He snorted a laugh, as he thought this was clever.

"Shut it, Pig!" snapped Grundy, shoving him.

Pig's smile turned into a scowl.

"What secret?" Grundy asked.

"Well...Isabella has made a new friend," Hortense began, "and he's a *monster* from the sea."

Grundy and Pig pricked up their ears. "Go on," said Grundy.

"He has a horn growing right out of his forehead. He's not a human; he's a narwhal boy. We saw him at the carnival by the sea."

"I heard he's a freak," said Pig.

"Yes, a horrible freak," replied Hortense. "But his horn is quite valuable, like the horn of a rhino or the tusk of an elephant."

The rusty gears of Grundy Bunion's brain began to turn. "Yeah…that would be some prize," he said.

"Yeah, like the *musk* of an elephant," snorted Pig.

"And *I* know how we can catch him," said Hortense.

"But you're just a worm eater," sneered Pig.

"That's enough out of you," said Grundy as he grabbed Pig by the collar and shoved him back into the trunk. He closed the lid and sat on it.

"Now, where were we, Cousin Hortense?" said Grundy.

She sat down next to him on the trunk's lid and whispered her plot.

* * *

Through a small hole in the tent that cloaked his tank, Bucky watched the moon's reflection dance in the waves. How he longed to swim in the ocean, the one place he truly felt at home. *If I cannot belong on land, I will belong to the sea*, he thought.

But this seemed hopeless, for Mr. Barker kept the iron gate locked tight atop Bucky's tank. And so he did what he was born to do—he swam back and forth and round and round the tank, an endless distance

carrying him nowhere. And in his mind, one word—
the name of the girl who kept the ever-dwindling spark
of hope alive in his heart, the one person in all the world
who neither pitied nor feared nor hated him—Isabella,
Isabella, Isabella.

"Psssst!" Suddenly the moon was gone—someone, or
some*thing*, was standing just outside the tent.

Bucky's heart raced. "Who…who's there?" he
whispered.

"I've come to free you," a boy's voice whispered back.

"W-Who a-are y-you?" stammered Bucky.

"A friend," said the voice.

"I don't have any friends," said Bucky, very suspicious now.

"You have one," said the voice.

"Oh yeah? And who is that?" said Bucky.

"Why, Isabella, of course."

Bucky's heart leaped. *Am I dreaming? Can this really be?*

A knife slashed the canvas tent, and the boy appeared, a lantern in one hand. "My name is Grundy,
Grundy Bunion. Isabella is waiting for you; we have to
move quickly."

Bucky stared at the young man in his ragged
clothes and black cap, wearing a strange grin that made

Bucky shiver. *What should I do?* he thought. He stared at the iron gate above and the glass walls of his tank. He thought about the days and months and years ahead that he would spend as Bucky the Narwhal Boy. He had no choice but to trust his alleged rescuer.

"I'm locked in," Bucky said.

The boy put down his lantern and flashed a bit of twisted wire. "I came prepared," he said. A few minutes later, he opened the lock and lifted the iron gate.

After Bucky climbed out, Grundy held the lantern close to Bucky's face and stared at the horn. It was the most unusual thing he'd ever seen, a long nautilus spiral, with pearly hues, gleaming in the lantern light. Visions of the wealth this horn would bring flashed in Grundy's mind.

"We should hurry," said Bucky. "Mr. Barker will kill both of us on the spot if he wakes up."

"Come this way."

Grundy grabbed Bucky's arm, and they crept out of the tent. When it was safe to run, they rushed to a pier that was far down the beach.

* * *

"You want to see her, don't you?" said Grundy.

"Yes, but this is a fishing boat; it's meant to go out to sea," said Bucky, cautious of the small vessel heaped with piles of netting at one end.

"And it's quiet, so Barker won't hear your escape," replied Grundy.

Bucky was suspicious. "But Isabella lives on land…"

"Yes…on an *island*. You haven't seen the ferry boats?" said Grundy.

"I'm not from here, wherever *here* is," said Bucky.

"Well, they don't run at night; that's why we're going in this one. Now, Barker will be after us any minute, so do you want to leave, or don't you?"

"All right," said Bucky, wagering that nothing could be worse than ending up back in the tank. He stepped down into the boat.

"Now, that's the spirit," said Grundy, flashing the strange grin that had given Bucky chills back in the tent. Grundy unmoored the boat and began rowing it across the calm tide. "It won't be long now," he said.

Grundy rowed and rowed, and Bucky saw no land in sight. "Where are we going?" Bucky said nervously.

"The island, silly. Where Isabella lives."

"All I see is open water."

"Look, there it is," said Grundy, pointing.

"Where?" said Bucky, searching the horizon.

"Right ahead of us, silly."

"I don't see any—" Bucky turned, but it was too late.

What followed blinked by in flashes. The pile of netting rose up like a waking sea monster. An oar sliced the damp, salty air and clipped Bucky behind the ear. Falling back into the boat, Bucky saw a person emerge from the netting, as an arm raised high in the air. At the end of the arm—a hand wielding a large knife. Bucky tried to stand, but the sky and ocean were swirling now, and he collapsed backward, hitting his head on the wooden seat.

"Watch the horn, you dope!" Bucky heard one of them say. And as he tried to stand, the oar came down again, knocking the wind out of him. The knife caught the moon's light. It was gleaming and polished to a mirror shine, and reminded Bucky of the scimitar that Sheik Qamar swallowed as one of Barker's other wonderments of nature.

The knife swept through the air, taking in its pass the thing that Bucky had so resented, the thing that had tipped the math out of his favor and made him different, made him a narwhal boy. Grundy Bunion held the horn in his greedy fist.

Through his blurring vision, Bucky saw it for the first time, outside of seeing its reflection. And Bucky smiled, for he saw in that final second how magnificent it was.

A third and final thud of the oar made everything go black and silent, so that Bucky did not even feel his body splash and sink—down, down, down—into the cold deep.

CHAPTER ELEVEN

The Picture Island

This world was cold, the sky heavy and gray. To the four lost extra children, everything seemed dead.

"It's not far now," said the white buffalo carrying the children on his broad back.

"I'm hungry," said Ant, "but what are we going to eat?"

"We will start a fire with stones and kindling, and the sea eagle will bring fish," said the white buffalo.

"Does he talk too?" asked Sally.

"Not he…she," said the white buffalo. "And not often, no. But like all animals, we understand one another."

"Well, I hope fish is better than creamed leaves," said Penny.

"The plants," said Buster, noticing the brittle stems and naked branches around him, "they're all dead."

"Not dead…dormant," said the white buffalo. "They're waiting, as are all things here."

"Waiting for what?" asked Buster.

Here, the white buffalo stopped, and his head drooped with a sigh. "For the dreams to come back," he said sadly. "They're waiting for their princess to return." The white buffalo resumed his lumbering walk.

A few moments later, they arrived at the mouth of a cave. Once inside, Penny and Buster started a fire while the white buffalo lay down with Ant and Sally to keep them warm. As the fire danced to life, a loud call from the sea eagle echoed throughout the cave. The sea eagle swooped in and dropped two plump fish at Penny's feet, causing her to yelp, and soared off.

"You want to know where you are and how you got here," said the white buffalo as the four hungry refugees devoured the fish. The fire was warming them, and their clothes were beginning to dry.

"Yes, that would be a good place to start," said Buster.

"Excuse me, Mr. Buffalo," said Sally between bites, "but we don't know your name."

"She's right," added Penny. "We haven't introduced ourselves. I'm Penny."

"I'm Ant."

"I'm Buster."

"And I'm Sally. We are from the—"

"Bunion Home for Extra Children," said the white buffalo, finishing Sally's sentence.

"But...how did you know that?" asked Buster, astonished.

The white buffalo stood and walked to the mouth of the cave, staring into the distance beyond. "This island was once a paradise," he said, "but now it is plagued by old hatreds and shameful memories."

Sally joined the white buffalo and stroked his leg. "From there?"

"Yes, Sally, it began long ago at your orphan home."

"Miss Bunion," muttered Ant and Penny in unison.

"Miss Bunion indeed," said the white buffalo. "It is by her dark magic that this island withers in decay."

"She's very mean to us," whispered Sally to him.

"We *hate* her," added Ant.

"Is she a witch?" asked Penny.

The white buffalo let out a long, slow breath and stared into the fire. "Her powers are great, and her heart a cold black stone," he said. "Her wicked curse reigns over all."

A chill raised the hairs on the back of the orphans' necks.

"I don't believe in witches," said Buster. "And I'm sure there's a logical solution if we think hard enough."

"There is another whose spirit is pure," said the white buffalo. "It is she who will set free this island... but, first, she must be found."

"The princess," said Sally.

The white buffalo nodded.

"You're a buffalo," said Buster. "How do you know all this?"

"As I said, I was not always as you see me." The white buffalo raised his head, exposing the snowy fur of his broad chest. "Now, gather close to the fire, and I will tell you the whole story."

* * *

Long before she met Bucky, Isabella spent hours dreaming up the world with a magic of her own invention. Most of the time, she could be found in the forest behind their large house, playing at an odd outcropping of rocks. This was her favorite place.

Her sister, Hortense, hated Isabella, for Hortense believed that Isabella stole all their father's love and left none for her. Hortense did not understand love, which is very much like the water in a river—going on forever without running out. What Hortense *did* understand was spite, pettiness, and anger. She practiced these often, and as with anything, practice makes perfect.

Hortense was jealous of Isabella's imaginary friends, of the pretend trips she took, and even of the tortoise that Isabella rode, the one Isabella had invented from a rock. Hortense did none of these things because she could not dream. And it was this that Hortense hated most of all in others—the ability to dream.

Hortense and Isabella lived in the large Bunion Home with their father, Osiris Bunion. A mapmaker, Osiris traveled to the farthest edges of the world and brought back the most exotic gifts—bracelets made from polished shells, or a totem pole carved from whalebone. But the most unusual gift of all was one of his own making—a map of infinite complexity, painted in the finest detail. Within the painted map, strange creatures appeared to leap out of the deep-blue brushstroke waves. Across the canvas, fine lines crisscrossed in arcs and circles like spun gold. A verdant island gleamed like an emerald from the center of the painting.

As a tool for orientation, it was flawless—every angle and distance was described with exacting detail and precision. And yet, it was also a map to a place that did not exist. But how could this be? To answer that, we must turn to the story of No Place Island.

* * *

For as long as there have been explorers traveling the oceans of the world, there have been tales of No Place Island. Voyagers have searched from one end of the earth to the other to find it, the Place of No Place, where every tree bears plump fruit, and granted wishes are as plentiful as sand. It was said that one lived forever on No Place Island, and that each step there led toward eternity.

Of course, this was a legend, a folk tale, as no one had ever found No Place Island. But that did not stop travelers from trying. Year after year, and decade after decade, explorers spent their lives in search of it. Just as those before them who had searched the sea for mermaids or sea dragons, their quests always ended in vain.

While the island could not be *found*, it could be *discovered*—if one was not expecting it. Osiris Bunion happened not to be looking for No Place Island the day that it appeared out of nowhere on a calm blue sea. Osiris, transfixed by the sight of it, knew this must be the impossible island, the Place of No Place. He stepped onto its shore and found himself in paradise. Time passed as it does in dreams—as if it were a pool he was floating in—and Osiris wanted to stay there forever. But he had a wife and two young daughters whom he loved very much. So after his exploration, Osiris bade farewell to the magic island and began his journey back home. His count of the sun's cycles told him that he had been away for two weeks. But when he arrived, his daughters were a full two years older than when he left. And his wife, sadly, had already taken her place in the Bunion family graveyard deep in the woods behind the Bunion Home.

Because Osiris was a mapmaker, he had a sharp eye for detail and the keen memory of an elephant. And in those early days of grief over his wife's passing, he lost himself in his work. He scribbled pages and pages of notes, and filled his sketchbook with drawings. He shut himself up in the attic of the Bunion home and painted for ten days and ten nights. And this was how the fantastic and strange painting of No Place Island came to be. He then began building the painting's thick wooden frame, carving rolling waves and exotic sea creatures at its edges.

Looking at the final product, Osiris saw that it was the greatest map he had ever made. What he didn't know—and what he never would have dreamed of—was how well it functioned.

* * *

"And so the mapmaker returned home to his children and his large house," concluded the white buffalo as the fire burned down to embers. "For days on end, he painted, and that is how the impossible map to an unreal place came to be."

"And this is the frame?" asked Buster, holding up the wooden rectangle they had pieced together in the stone room.

"Yes," said the white buffalo.

"But where is the picture?" asked Penny.

The white buffalo lowered his head in thought. "I fear that the only person who knows the answer to that is Hortense Bunion herself."

Their faces froze.

"You see," the white buffalo continued, "the mapmaker had two little girls, Hortense and Isabella."

"But then, all this must have happened a long time ago," said Ant, "since Miss Bunion is at least a hundred years old now."

"Yes, it was a long time ago," replied the white buffalo. "But magic, good or bad, never dies. And the power of her evil only grows stronger with age."

"What about Isabella and the mapmaker?" asked Sally.

The white buffalo's chest rose and fell with a deep breath. "They succumbed to the trickery and black sorcery of Hortense herself."

Sally gasped, her eyes wide. "So she really is a witch!"

"She acquired great power through stolen magic," said the white buffalo. "Enchantment, robbed and swindled, then poisoned with all the anger in her cold heart."

A shiver snuck up each of the orphans' arms, leaving a trail of goose bumps.

"But why?" asked Sally. "How did she get to be so mean?"

"Hortense was jealous of her sister, Isabella. So much so that her hatred pushed every other thought from her mind and feeling from her heart."

"So what happened to Isabella?" asked Ant.

It was hard for the orphans to tell, but if animals were capable of tears, then surely that is what they saw in the eyes of the white buffalo.

"She is still here," he said softly, "somewhere on this island. Shrouded, hidden by the curse of her spiteful sister." The white buffalo lowered his eyes. "I have looked every day for her over these many years. But my beloved Isabella has never been found."

One by one, understanding dawned on the faces of the four extra children.

"You mean—" began Buster.

"Yes," interrupted the white buffalo, looking deeply into each of their faces. "I am their father. I am Osiris Bunion."

CHAPTER TWELVE

Treasures
Lost and Found

T he world of the deep—thick, cold, silent—was new and strange. Blue faded to black and back again. This was how the days passed. But there was no time here, none that mattered at least. Only movement, the constant flow of life streaming through the iridescent depths. The sea was not as Bucky remembered it. But how far had he come since first plunging from his father's fishing boat?

Here, he was among them, one of them, as he thought he had wanted to be. And he was shed of his horn, finally normal. But normal to whom? Him? The shivering tides? He couldn't say, but it meant nothing here anyway.

Three wishes Bucky had made, and three were granted. First, a wish to be free—to escape the tank under the sign which read, "THE AMAZING NARWHAL

BOY." Second, a wish to return to the sea, a place he once felt at home. And third, a wish to be rid of his defect, the mutation jutting from his forehead whose magnificence he'd lost faith in. He had only truly seen his horn, glinting in the moonlight, after it was taken by the swift knife slashing the night sky.

Three wishes—all granted. And yet there was a fourth wish—her name was Isabella. *How curious,* thought Bucky, *that this final wish is now made impossible by the granting of the first three!*

* * *

"BURGLED BEAST BEWILDERS BARKER," shouted the headline of the newspaper Grundy Bunion held in his fist. Hortense locked the attic door behind him. "Well, I see you've actually done it," she said, her eyes feasting on the newsprint. "Impressive, certainly."

Grundy sneered with satisfaction. "Yeah, everything went according to plan."

"Yeah, *apporting to clan,*" snorted Pig.

Hortense snatched the newspaper from Grundy and continued reading. "Indeed, it did—though it seems a Mr. Cornelius Barker is not too happy about your success," she warned. "It appears this Narwhal Boy was his prize attraction."

The grubby faces of Grundy and Pig flickered with worry. "Humph…he don't know nuthin'," grunted Pig.

"That's right. We was real quiet—he didn't see a thing," boasted Grundy.

Hortense shook her head doubtfully. "Well…he *is* offering a large reward." She raised one eyebrow. "It's a good thing that the Narwhal Boy's misfortune is *our* little secret."

Grundy's filthy palms began to sweat. "Yeah… our little secret." *What is Hortense up to?* he wondered.

Hortense folded the newspaper and tossed it aside. "Well then…show me the souvenir you've brought back from your little boat ride."

Grundy peered out the window to be sure there were no unexpected visitors on the way. He nodded to Pig, who unwrapped the treasure from a battered satchel.

It was even more dazzling than Hortense had remembered. A perfect spiral lancing the air with shifting colors that seemed liquid in the light. Her eyes danced with wicked curiosity as she snatched it up with both hands. "Thank you," she snapped, "that will be all, Cousin."

Grundy and Pig stared at one another, slack-jawed. "*What* did you say?" Grundy asked, seething.

"I *said*, that will be all—kindly leave now."

Pig hadn't yet caught on, but Grundy's face turned red with anger. "Not without this, I'm not!" He grabbed the horn, but Hortense wouldn't let go.

"You must be joking," she said as they struggled.

"IT'S HALF MINE!" shouted Grundy. "WE HAD A DEAL!"

Pig looked back and forth between them, confused.

"Keep your voice down!" said Hortense. "*I* don't remember any deal."

"I smell a ratfish," said Pig.

"Well, I'm not leaving here without it!" said Grundy.

It dawned on Pig that he might be getting the short end—or more correctly, no end—of this bargain. Though quite dumb in most regards, greed in any form was one thing Pig had no trouble understanding. Pig punched Grundy in the arm.

Grundy let go of the horn as he turned to Pig. "Hey…what's the idea, punchin' me?"

"Half yours, half hers, half mine—*that* wuzza deal."

Grundy shoved him, and Pig kicked Grundy in the shin.

Hortense watched their scuffle with bored indifference, as if they were two bugs she would soon step on. "Very well," she began, her voice suddenly sweet, "you may have it. I will have to settle for Mr. Barker's handsome reward once I tell him what happened to his poor Narwhal Boy."

Grundy and Pig froze. "You can't—you wouldn't dare!" cried Grundy. "It was all *your* idea anyway!"

Hortense's face melted into pure innocence. "That will be *your* story. Of course, *mine* will be much different." She smiled. "But I wonder who will be believed— a sweet, young angel or two nasty boys who have been nothing but trouble since the day they were born?"

Grundy's head slumped; he realized she had them.

Pig's face was a question mark. "Whazat mean?" he whined.

Grundy smacked Pig in the head.

"Oow!" Pig moaned.

"It means you're an idiot!" said Grundy. "Now, shut up and come on!" He glared at Hortense before slamming the door behind him.

She held her bounty up to the light, traced the spiraling horn with one finger, and let out a terrible laugh.

* * *

Bucky was lost in the infinite sea—in every direction he looked, the same blue field stretched out forever. And at the surface, a line of blue sky meeting blue water—an endless circle unbroken by land. Every day he rose to the surface, felt the breeze of salty air on his face, and searched the horizon for land. He dreamed of finding the beach with the carousel and watching Isabella wave from her white horse.

Every day he looked, and every day his eyes met only the flat blue horizon. And as the days disappeared like raindrops into the bottomless pool of time, Bucky's hopes of finding Isabella slowly crumbled and fell away. Who was he now, since he'd lost his horn and was no longer the Narwhal Boy? And *why* was he? Bucky had no answers.

He remembered the days in his father's fishing boat and the first time he'd sliced the water with his horn. How agile and quick he had been! Leaping and diving as if the sea were air and he a soaring eagle. In that ocean, so long ago and far away, Bucky had known true freedom. But now he merely gave himself to the random tides. It was the horn growing from his forehead that had allowed Bucky to swim so deftly; without it, he was clumsy, heavy, and slow. The water now seemed a foreign place. It no longer mattered if he was on land or sea—everywhere, he was a stranger and utterly alone.

Bucky was lost and tired. And on one cold gray day, he did not swim to the surface to look for Isabella. Instead, he gave himself to the overwhelming sea and his own heart heavy with loss. Bucky closed his eyes and took the water deep into himself, his body slack with indifference, and drifted down into the abyss.

CHAPTER THIRTEEN

The Opened Trunk

It pained Ursa to see the hungry orphans sent to bed with no supper, but now there were four lost extra children to be found—a missed meal was the least of her worries. Ursa bundled herself in three layers of clothing, lit a lantern, and headed out into the black night in search of Penny, Buster, Sally, and Ant. She tried not to think about how cold it was or how long they had been out in it. Many years ago, two others had ventured from this house into the frozen woods, never to return. "Two's plenty enough for this icy forest," she prayed silently to herself. "Please spare us four more."

* * *

As Ursa trudged through the snow, Miss Bunion was also preparing to find the four missing extra children. But she did not look to the frigid trees stretching endlessly beyond the Bunion Home. Instead, her ancient, crooked fingers were now unclasping the tarnished hasp of the old wooden trunk up in her attic graveyard of forgotten things.

A torrent of memories flooded Miss Bunion's mind as she strained to lift the trunk's heavy lid. At the side of the trunk, the tattered scroll fluttered violently as if in protest to her actions. So old was her dark magic! And so many years since the trunk had been opened! And the painted map, torn so carelessly from its frame— how long since eyes had seen it? How long since anyone had gazed at its perfect lines and fallen under its mysterious spell?

* * *

While Isabella often stared deeply in wonder at her father's magnificent map, he had no idea that she *used* it as well. When Osiris left on long trips, drawing routes to the far corners of the world, Isabella spent days in the attic with the painted map—she called it the picture island—whose title was *The Place of No Place*. Because Isabella could dream, the map painting served its intended purpose. Isabella traveled through the picture to the legendary island gone undiscovered by so many explorers over so many lifetimes. For if one believed strongly enough in their wishes, the painted map would swirl and fall away, revealing the island itself beneath a cloudless blue sky.

On Isabella's first journey, she wondered how she would return to her world. As she thought this, a sea eagle swooped down, picked her up, and flew her to the top of a hill overlooking the island. There, she found a massive rock fortress—the sea eagle told her this was the Castle of the Infinite Domain. In this castle, a stone room housed a long table and chairs, and a tall mirror set into one wall. This was a special mirror, for it reflected not a person's face, but rather their soul. If one's spirit was pure, the eagle explained, then the glass swirled and melted away, leaving a field of clouds within a blue sky. If one was wicked, then the mirror became a slab of black stone. It was through this mirror that those of pure spirit could return to the known world.

Isabella didn't ask the eagle what happened to those who tried to pass through the black stone, so she couldn't answer when Hortense asked her. Isabella was hoping her sister would join her in this strange and wondrous place, as she thought it might cheer her up. And so she told Hortense of her journeys to the picture island. But Hortense never ventured through the magic frame.

Perhaps it was the mystery of the mirror that kept Hortense from following her sister to the picture island. Whatever the reason, her jealous hatred of Isabella only grew because of her inability to experience the secret realm. But one day Hortense would show her—she would get even with Isabella for all that she reaped from her kind heart, all that Hortense herself could never obtain through her own envy and spite.

A few weeks later, the sisters would go to the carnival by the sea, ride the carousel, and see the grotesque boy swimming in his tank. And this Narwhal Boy would be the key to all the terrible events that followed… events that haunted her and the Bunion Home all these years hence.

* * *

But now, the rusty hinges of the old trunk groaned as Miss Bunion threw open the lid. There in the trunk sat the thing that had been so hideous to the world, but seemed magnificent only when freed from its owner. Miss Bunion's bony fingers reached into the trunk and plucked out the Narwhal Boy's stolen horn. It tingled in her wrinkled palm as she cackled with pleasure.

It was here in this attic, so many years ago, that she first discovered the power of the magical spire. Isabella was in the attic, as usual, when Hortense marched up the steps with her surprise. Isabella was writing something on the back of the picture's frame when Hortense burst in. She wasted no time in pulling out the treasure for Isabella to see. Words were not necessary, as the sight of the thing itself told its own story.

"No…" was all Isabella could say when she realized what her sister held. She dropped her pen and rushed to grab the horn, but Hortense yanked it out of her reach as her taunting laughter stabbed the air. "You can't…you didn't…" sobbed Isabella.

Hortense drew slow circles with the horn, and the air in the attic became chilly and electric. Isabella wondered if the tears were distorting her vision as her sister, Hortense, seemed to turn the faintest shade of green.

Hortense's laughter stopped suddenly, and her face screwed into a scowl. Her eyes were now black. Isabella was used to feeling sad for her sister, but she had never feared her until now. The point of the horn, glowing now, made hypnotic spirals in the air. Hortense's tongue traced her lips; it was black now—the tongue of a snake. Isabella froze, disbelieving her sister's transformation.

"Iiiiiiiccccceee..." the word left Hortense's green lips as a slow hiss. "Iiiiiiiicccccceeee..." Isabella didn't notice that Hortense had opened the picture map with this spell, or that a black fog was overtaking the painted island. "Iiiiiiccccceee..." Hortense hissed again.

Isabella stepped backward. She could see her breath in the chilled attic air.

"Iiiiiccccceee...aaaaaaahhh...bell...ah..." Hortense intoned. "Iiicccee...ahhh...bellahhh." Then a third and final time, "Iccee..ah..BELLA!"

A frozen tornado burst through the black fog within the frame and swallowed Isabella.

* * *

"Ice-a-bella," said old Miss Bunion to herself, snaking a crooked finger down the horn that had been locked away all these many years. Ice-a-bella, the curse that had sent her sister into the chilling wind of the picture island, never to return. And it was this word, with a wave of the stolen horn, that had left the paradise a frozen ruin.

The iridescent horn seemed to hum in Hortense's hands. "Now do you see?" she cackled to the scrolled canvas at her feet. It ruffled as if in a gale. With a wave of the horn, the picture map rose up and unfurled itself in midair. "Ice-a-bella and old buffalo, trapped in your wasteland—your warm hearts are no match for the cold I bring!"

On these last words, the picture island turned gray, and its bordering sea swirled with violent whirlpools. A dark fog swallowed the painting as shooting bolts of frozen air burst forth from the canvas, peppering the attic floor with ice and snow.

Miss Bunion's face wrinkled into a green prune. Frigid ocean waters crashed through the map, sending tendrils of seaweed and kelp into the tangled gray of her wiry hair. Miss Bunion stood firm in the pounding wind, as it was the key to her transformation. She spat black crows of laughter and gave herself over to the furious gusts flying from the cursed picture map. A hand, now green and scaled, reached for the snowy dome on the shelf. She flung the globe into the map, and it disappeared without a sound.

"Ten horses!" she shouted into the tornado. "Ten horses to my dark purpose! Ice-a-bella must not be found!"

And with those words, the Sea Witch that was Miss Bunion leaped into the tornado and was cast forth into her blighted world.

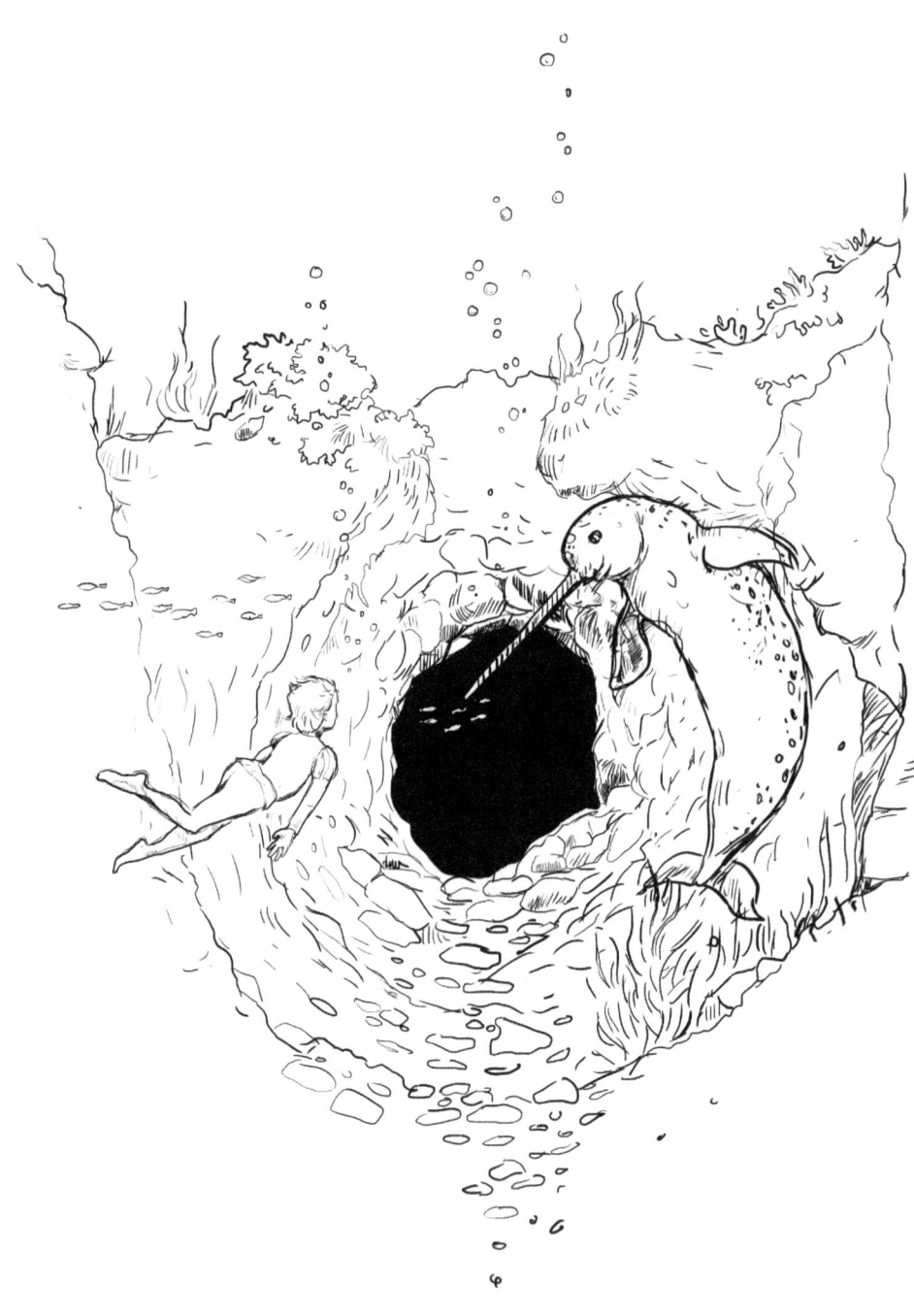

CHAPTER FOURTEEN

The Deep

The depth of the sea had no end, and Bucky thought he would sink forever. Blue water turned to indigo then deepest black. He was overtaken by a sleep without dreams, falling ever downward with no purpose or destination, an endless dying.

He finally reached the ocean floor, which was not death but rather a strange new place. It was dark here, and he could hardly make out the glowing eels and fish that swam by. His eye caught something familiar that gave off a faint light there at the bottom of the ocean. It was a long spiral that ended in a great lumbering body. Here before him was the creature he had seen so long ago in the library and in Mr. Barker's dusty book—the thing he had once thought himself to be. Here before Bucky at the bottom of the ocean was the narwhal itself. *What are the words Mr. Barker used? Monodon monoceros. Horned whale. Narwhal, Prince of the Sea.*

The terms swam in Bucky's head as the massive creature drifted toward him, but Bucky was too shocked to move.

"Heelllooo." The sound came from the spired whale, in waves traveling through the water, and reverberated in Bucky's head. "I have been waiting many tides for you to arrive here."

Bucky looked at the horn, which even in the depths shimmered with every color imaginable. It was just like the one he'd lost. "What…or who…are you?" Bucky asked.

"You don't know me," said the creature, "and I am to blame for that."

"Are you…the narwhal?"

"Now and forever, but not always so," said the narwhal. "You see, it was *I* who did not know *you,* and that is why I am now…as you see me."

Bucky stared with curiosity and wonder. "I know what you are. You are a narwhal. I once had a horn like yours, though I lived on land, and it only brought me sadness." Bucky swam closer to the narwhal. "Only when I lost my horn did I understand."

"Understand what?"

"That it was what made me magnificent."

The huge mammal turned so his wide eye was staring into Bucky's own. "I too lost something of great value," said the narwhal.

"Did you lose your horn once too? I wondered if mine would grow back."

"It was not my horn that I lost. It was something far greater."

"What could be worse for a narwhal than losing his horn?"

"I lost my son. My son...Bucky."

"No—it can't be."

"It is true—I am your father."

"But how...why?"

"I was out in my boat; you were high on the cliff," said the narwhal. "I saw you leave with a carnival barker. I feared I would never see you again. I was right."

"I didn't belong in the village," said Bucky. "So I became a wonderment of nature. I'm sorry, Father."

"I pushed you away, all because you were different—the boy with a horn."

"I don't understand...you're a human, not a narwhal," said Bucky.

"Weeks passed, and I prayed that you would come back. I searched the water, looking for a sign of you. But you were not to be found on water or land." The narwhal's horn swept back and forth slowly as he shook his head in regret. "My grief turned to anger, and instead of praying, I cursed the heavens. At that moment, the sky turned black and poured out an angry storm. A wave overtook my boat, and I fell into the sea. There, I awoke from a deep sleep—no longer human, but a narwhal."

Bucky looked deep into the narwhal's large eye. "I see you," he said finally.

"To find you, I was made...like you," explained the Narwhal.

"Oh, Father."

"Yours, yes, and may you forgive me for being so."

Bucky placed his hand on the narwhal's mottled-gray body. "I once met a girl who showed me only kindness. She didn't think I was a freak. Her name was Isabella."

"Love is not kindness," admitted the Narwhal, " and I was not kind to you. Yet I cannot undo what has been done."

Bucky pressed his cheek to the narwhal's body. "I forgive you. For Isabella, I forgive you."

The narwhal brought his head to Bucky's face, and for a moment they were silent.

The narwhal's eye widened as he finally spoke, "Come. Your journey is not yet done."

"But where are we going?"

"To the Cave of the Deep."

* * *

As they swam across the vast ocean floor, Bucky told his father about his life as Cornelius Barker's Narwhal Boy and how he met Isabella, who had shown him neither malice nor fear. He recounted his escape and demise at the hands of Grundy Bunion on that terrible night. "And then I became a creature of the deep, as you are," Bucky explained. "But without my horn, I am clumsy and slow in the water. I looked and looked for the carousel by the beach, hoping to find Isabella again."

"And now, here you are," said his father.

"I never found her. I never found the carousel. So I shut my eyes and let the sea take me—" Bucky stopped, as they were at the mouth of an immense black chasm. "Father, what is this?"

"The Cave of the Deep."

"But why have you brought me here?"

"From your despair will come understanding," is all the narwhal answered. He pointed with his horn to the dark waters inside the cave. "Go."

"Father, wh-what's in th-there?" stammered Bucky.

"You, your nature. See it with a pure spirit, and you shall know your destiny."

Bucky was frightened. "Come with me, Father."

The narwhal's horn swept slowly from side to side. "I cannot—only *you* can see your true nature."

The blackness of the Cave of the Deep seemed to stretch on forever. "I don't want to go."

"Go you must," his father said. "There is no other way."

"Way? For what?"

The narwhal brought his enormous eye close to Bucky's own. "For you to live again."

Once inside the Cave of the Deep, Bucky was wrapped in darkness. Time was impossible to measure, and it seemed hours before he could see or hear anything. But onward he swam, deeper and deeper into the cave. Finally, he reached a room; the walls of the cave grew high and trapped a large mass of air, creating a cathedral above the sea-lake. As Bucky's head broke the surface, he found he could breathe the air as he had done on land. The room glowed with a golden light that seemed to come from Bucky himself.

Bucky pulled himself to the edge of the lake. The rock wall was polished smooth, and Bucky stared at himself, for the first time seeing the stump where his horn had been.

But then Bucky's image melted away from the polished stone, and a vision of Isabella on the carousel swirled into view. Then the sight of Mr. Barker locking the heavy iron gate atop his tank. This too faded and was replaced by the sight of an old white buffalo chewing seagrass on a gray beach. Then the image of a horrible witch with kelp for hair, wielding the very horn that had grown out of Bucky's own forehead. Then Isabella appeared beside the witch as the witch pointed his stolen horn at Isabella. The witch cackled, waving the horn and drawing up a great wind.

And then Isabella was gone.

Bucky bolted from the cave, swimming back out as fast as he could.

* * *

Weeks had passed since Bucky left the Cave of the Deep and bid farewell to his father, the narwhal. The cave had shown him his purpose—he must find Isabella and save her from the witch who had stolen his horn. He prayed it was not already too late.

He swam for days, and his body was spent. But Bucky could not afford weariness or exhaustion. So on he swam, combing the sea and searching the horizon in hopes of finding the shore with the carousel...and Isabella waving from the white horse.

When he had nearly given up, his eyes found a rainbow of colors sparkling above the water. For a day, he swam toward it. Under a clear sky, he glimpsed the carousel, a jewel set in the beach. The next day, he was closer still. Squinting, he could just make out the hand of Isabella waving from her white horse. There was nothing else—no carnival or wonderments of nature—just Isabella and her circling animals.

"Tomorrow," Bucky said to himself, "Tomorrow I will arrive at the shore. I will purge the water from my lungs and take deep breaths of the salty sea air. I will walk to Isabella not as Narwhal Boy but as a person, a human...and she will be there waiting."

The next day, the sky was gray, and it spit an icy wind. A thunderstorm soaked the beach, and Bucky swam as fast as he could. Reaching the shore, he ran on unfamiliar legs to the carousel—now ruined and laid to waste on the frigid sand. Isabella was nowhere to be found.

Bucky went to the white horse, now covered in kelp and seagrass. He pulled the debris away and cast it onto the beach, as if to free the wooden animal. Then he did so with the rest of the animals, now half buried in the wet sand.

And though the kelp and seagrass returned with the tides, Bucky came back the next day to clear the animals of the sea's waste.

And he would do the same tomorrow…and tomorrow… and every tomorrow hence…for surely one tomorrow Isabella would return.

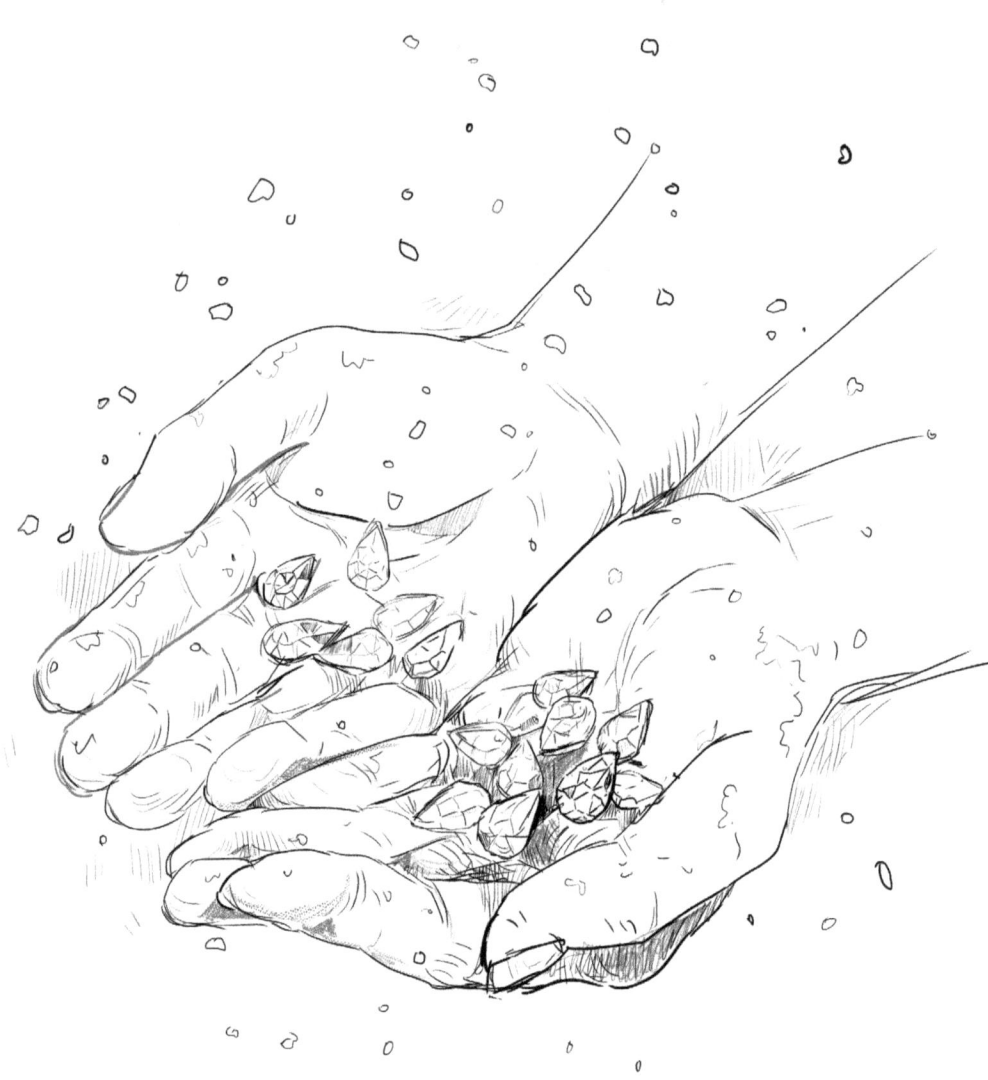

CHAPTER FIFTEEN

Ice-a-bella

N ight was falling, and frosty air swept through the cave. Osiris Bunion, the old white buffalo, stared across the dying fire into the faces of Sally, Ant, Penny, and Buster.

Buster was the first to speak. "If you're their father," he began thoughtfully, "then it was *you* who painted the map?"

"Yes. I found No Place Island quite by accident on one of my travels. It was I who painted the picture map that has brought so much ruin to this land."

"But you are a buffalo," said Sally.

"Yes, now and evermore, but not before," he replied.

"You said that Miss Bunion cursed her sister and her father," said Penny.

"By stolen magic," added Ant.

Osiris nodded gravely.

"So Miss Bunion turned you into a buffalo?" asked Sally.

"Through her black magic and trickery, yes," he replied. "Buster, fetch a log for the fire. There is much to tell you." And the white buffalo, Osiris, knelt in the cave and began his tale of the terrible events that happened so long ago at the Bunion Home.

* * *

In the creaking attic of the Bunion Home, young Hortense laid down the stolen horn and stared into the painted map that swirled with fog. A moment before, she had cursed her sister with the word *Ice-a-bella* said three times with a wave of the pearly staff. Hortense craned her head and peered into the frame with grim fascination. She watched Isabella fall—the freezing winds wrapping her in a cocoon of ice—and then her sister was gone, lost in the wilderness of the ruined picture island. How many times had Hortense endured Isabella's tales of this place? Of the magic carousel that ran on dreams, or the Castle of the Infinite Domain?

"As long as the carousel turns, all is well in the picture world," Isabella had explained.

Hortense had now put an end to that, for the carousel lay twisted and broken on the beach, the knife-cold winds gnawing at its crippled animals. Hortense smiled. She had taken the horn from the strange Narwhal Boy, and now she had taken away her sister's paradise. All of it seized by the bitterness of her own heart. Even her sister, her own flesh and blood, was now trapped forever on that condemned picture island.

In spite of all the cruelty she had already wrought, Hortense was not satisfied. If she had thought that her savage conjuring would bring a moment's happiness to her diabolical spirit, Hortense was sadly disappointed to find that it did not—for evil is a hungry beast whose stomach is never full.

Hortense raised the horn that was the agent of her wickedness. With violent stabs, she used it to rip the edges of the canvas, freeing the extraordinary picture map from its wooden gate. With crashing blows of the horn, she demolished the frame that her father had so carefully carved. She shoved the scrolled painting into a crevice in the attic wall and gathered the pieces of broken frame into an old blanket. Out she went, into the cold, to the deep woods and granite garden so loved by her sister. Crawling under a flat stone, she wedged the blanket between two slabs.

"Ursa!" cried Hortense, returning from the cold and hurrying to the kitchen. "Get father quickly! Isabella is lost in the woods—she'll freeze if we don't find her!" Ursuline was the chambermaid. And though only slightly younger than Hortense herself, Hortense treated Ursa as if she were a slave and not a fellow child.

Mr. Bunion is a kind man, thought Ursa, *and surely he will see to it that I am provided for and treated well.* She dreamed of escaping her servant post…but this was not to be.

"I'll look for Isabella while you get father. Hurry, you foolish wench!" shouted Hortense.

Ursa dropped the pot she was washing and wiped her hands on her skirt. "Yes, ma'am. Right away, ma'am," she replied and scurried out into the cold.

By the time that Ursa and Mr. Bunion got back to the Bunion Home, there was only an hour of daylight left to search for Isabella.

* * *

The memory of that cold night so long ago—the night that Isabella disappeared—was a ghost haunting Ursa all these many years. Now, as she trudged out in search of Ant, Penny, Buster, and Sally, Ursa's mind's eye saw Mr. Bunion venturing out through the deep snow in search of his daughter. Two were lost that terrible night, but only one was found.

It was Ursa who discovered him. Early the next morning, as the sun tempered the biting winds, she trekked out to the woods, to the place Isabella most loved to play. Flagstones poked through the snow, amid granite slabs as long as tables. Here rested the Bunions of three generations past, in this small family graveyard that was now overtaken by the forest. And there, sitting on the edge of a long granite vault, Ursa found Osiris Bunion.

He was utterly still and dusted with frost, as if he had turned to stone. Disbelieving her eyes, Ursa shook Mr. Bunion and pleaded for him to wake up. But his was the sleep from which there is no waking. The tears he had shed there, waiting for Isabella, had frozen while falling. They gathered as a heap of diamonds in his frozen hands. Ursa added her own tears to the cold snow as she shouted for him to wake up.

With Osiris and Isabella gone, it was Hortense alone to whom Ursa answered. As much as Mr. Bunion had been kind, compassionate, merciful, and generous, Hortense Bunion was doubly the opposite. Good will and virtue had no place in her tiny heart. Osiris Bunion had made generous provisions for Ursa in his will, though she never knew this—Hortense, being the sole remaining heir of the Bunion estate, had seen that those pages were ripped from Mr. Bunion's will. And so Ursa never escaped her lowly station, and remained in the service of Hortense Bunion all these years since.

"Not four more," prayed Ursa as she plodded through the deep snow in search of Buster, Penny, Ant, and Sally.

She neared the graveyard where she had found the frozen Mr. Bunion so many years ago. The newest headstone to grace this landscape read "Osiris Bunion." And engraved on the back, only one word—"Isabella."

* * *

While Ursa was trying to shake to life the cold body of Mr. Bunion, Hortense was in the attic, conducting her own investigation. Twice, she waved the cursed horn over Isabella's beloved snow dome. The carousel inside disappeared in a black soup of fog, which cleared to reveal the picture island, spoiled now by her wicked spell. And there, on the shore of the ruined picture island, she saw her shivering father. Hortense watched through the dome as he ran to the carousel, but Isabella wasn't there.

How bitter was the soul of Hortense Bunion and how unforgiving! That she would blight her family so, merely because she felt slighted in her father's love!

Twice more, the stolen horn passed over the glass dome, and her father was turned into a white buffalo. Hortense intended for him to join the circling parade of the other carousel animals, but her command of dark magic had not yet been mastered. And so the white buffalo was free to roam the cold island in search of Isabella.

Her malicious work done, Hortense placed the Narwhal Boy's horn in the old trunk and covered the snow dome with the black curtain. There they remained, undisturbed, all these many years hence.

That is, until the day that old Miss Bunion saw the four empty chairs in the dining room of the Bunion Home.

CHAPTER SIXTEEN

The Discovered Princess

With the strange and dreadful tale spinning in their heads, Buster, Ant, Penny, and Sally tried to sleep. But a crash of thunder broke the silence, and frigid air blasted through the cave and snuffed out the last of the fire.

The buffalo, Osiris, woke with a start and raised his broad head. He sensed a great evil was upon them. "Quickly," he exclaimed, "you must get back—she has discovered your presence here!" Osiris rose up and helped them onto his broad shoulders.

"Who?" asked Ant, sleepy and confused.

"The Sea Witch," said Osiris. "You are a danger to her—if Isabella is found, then the great power of her evil is threatened."

"We have to find Isabella!" said Sally bravely.

"Yes, we must save this place," agreed Buster, helping Sally onto Osiris's back.

"There's nothing we can do," said Penny, afraid. "We should go back through the mirror—we've been gone so long, and Ursa will be worried!"

"We can't go back now," said Sally. "We have to search for the princess!"

"The residents of this island are but shadows of the past," boomed Osiris. "Save yourselves, and worry not about this cursed place!"

"Looking at the math, five have a better chance of finding Isabella than one," offered Buster as he climbed onto Osiris's back.

"I agree—we should stay and find her!" said Ant.

"You will return to your realm, through the mirror in the Castle of the Infinite Domain!" shouted Osiris. "Now, hold tight to my mane—there is not much time!"

And they bolted into the gray, turbulent night.

As they traveled the ridge overlooking the beach, there was a great crash in the water. Osiris looked over the edge of the cliff, to the surf. He had underestimated her power, and what he saw quickened his heart. "She is here...and she is not alone," Osiris warned. "Hurry. Get down."

They leaped from the buffalo's back.

"Follow this path to the castle. I will distract her—you should have time to get there safely. Now run!"

"But we can't leave you," protested Buster.

With fire in his eyes, the old white buffalo reared up and bared his wide chest. "Do not question me!" he shouted. "Run for your lives!"

Shaken, the four extra children fled up the path.

* * *

The Sea Witch crashed into the cold ocean. Her face, now the color of algae, was lined with deep ridges, and her skin was covered in scales.

"Ten horses!" she commanded from the depths.

Ten black seahorses—each as tall as a man—swam to her. The largest lowered his neck, taking the Sea Witch onto his spiny back. And like a fearful army, they boiled up from the depths, into the shallows, and finally onto the shore.

The Sea Witch raised the long, spiraled horn in triumph, shaking it at the white buffalo who stared down from a high ridge above. She laughed her terrible laugh, for she saw the four misbegotten orphans hopping down from his back. With her ink-black cavalry in tow, she sped down the beach toward the path to the castle.

Deep in the dark waters, Bucky, too, felt a great evil announce itself. He raced to the surface and caught sight of the witch he had seen in the Cave of the Deep. A swarm of black seahorses followed behind, their slimy coats covered with sharp spikes. In the witch's hand, piercing the sky, was his own stolen horn. Bucky swam for the shore as fast as his body would take him.

The white buffalo, Osiris, thundered down the path toward the Sea Witch who, in another lifetime, had been his daughter Hortense. The Sea Witch and her aquatic steeds barreled toward him. Osiris got as far as the broken carousel before facing her.

With a wave of the Sea Witch's poisoned wand, the black seahorses halted.

"I have been waiting for you, Hortense," said Osiris.

"And I have looked forward to this reunion for many years, Father."

"Your powers are considerable—you must be very proud."

"I am, Father—not that you ever noticed."

"You were my daughter once, and I loved you as such. Only you were too blinded by jealousy to see it."

"Love!" thundered the Witch. "How dare you speak to me of love! Never did I get a drop!"

The heavy lids fell over Osiris's large eyes. "A drowned man has no use for air—such was my affection in the ocean of your envy!"

The witch's green skin glowed with rage. Lightning fired from her pilfered wand. "You loved her too much! Isabella stole you from me!"

Osiris hung his head in despair. Both daughters, for different reasons, were lost to him. "Isabella did you no wrong." His voice held no anger, only sadness. "My love was an ocean, an ocean dried to a raindrop by your jealousy and spite."

"I have no need for your raindrops, old buffalo!" she seethed.

"Nor did you ever," said Osiris, his voice breaking. "When I died, they were returned to me, unused, and gathered as frozen diamonds in my hands."

A silence followed, and for an instant, Osiris thought he saw the green fade from the Sea Witch's skin, and the face of his daughter return.

But the green hue flooded back into her cheeks as a howl roared from her mouth. Into the air went the cursed spire, and in a flash, her soldiers were upon him. The ten black seahorses trampled the white buffalo with their spiked tails, pounding him into the hard sand.

With their dark mission complete, the Sea Witch led her brigade up the path toward the extra children.

* * *

The sea eagle perched high in her nest on the other side of the island. She was about to tear into her lunch of wolffish when a terrible thunder rose from the shore below. Through narrowed eyes, she could just make out the white buffalo as he was overtaken by the black seahorses. Piercing the sky with a screaming cry, she dropped her wolffish and launched.

* * *

The anger in Osiris's voice startled the extra children. They quickly dismounted and began sprinting up the path.

When Penny stopped to catch her breath, she saw that there were only three of them. "Stop!" she cried. "Where's Sally?"

Their eyes darted in all directions. Sally was nowhere in sight.

"She was right behind me," said Ant.

"Footprints," said Buster, his eyes scanning the snow-covered ground. "We'll backtrack until we see where she broke off from us."

They raced back, eyes peeled for fresh tracks.

"Here!" shouted Ant, pointing to a trail of small footprints that led into the woods. "Come on!"

They followed Ant into the forest. "Sally? Sally!" they called.

And then Penny spotted her at the edge of an icy stream. "I've found her!" shouted Penny.

"I've found her!" shouted Sally.

"Sally! This is no time for echo tag!" Penny was annoyed at Sally's parroting. Since the extra children of the Bunion Home had no toys to play with, they made up their own games. Echo tag was one of Sally's favorites.

"No—*her!*" cried Sally. She pointed to a spot of tangled branches on the other side of the brook.

"What do you mean?" asked Ant. "I don't see anything."

"Sally, do you mean you found Isabella?" asked Buster.

"I *know* I have!" said Sally.

"We're wasting time; we have to get home!" snapped Penny.

"Look," said Ant, pointing to a tangled lump of leaves and twigs encased in ice. "I think Sally may have found something after all."

They all stared at the misshapen mass.

"Those are arms," said Sally.

"And I see a face," said Ant.

"Yes, I see it now too," said Buster.

"This is ridiculous," griped Penny. "I'm going to the castle."

"Go if you want," said Buster. "We're staying here."

Penny hated this trick. Buster knew as well as she did that going off alone was not the best idea at the moment. "Fine," she said. "We all stay for this goose chase."

Sally traced a frozen branch with her finger. "We need to take her to Osiris," she said.

"Yes, Osiris will know how to wake her up," said Ant.

"Right then, Ant and I should be able to lift her," said Buster.

They gently hoisted the mass of ice and branches from its crust of snow, and the four extra children headed to Osiris's cave.

They were on the high ridge.

"No," said Penny.

"What is it?" said Buster.

Penny was staring at the beach below as she pointed at a white figure lying beside the ruined carousel.

The truth stabbed them all like a slow knife—there on the sand was Osiris, motionless, his body crippled and twisted.

"The Sea Witch," said Sally.

"Maybe Isabella can save him," said Buster. "Quick, this way." Buster led the way down to the cold shore.

As they neared Osiris, they watched the young man from the sea—the strange boy who had so carefully cleaned the kelp and seagrass from the carousel animals—swim ashore. He knelt beside the buffalo. Sally and Penny rushed to Osiris as Buster and Ant followed with the ice princess.

* * *

The boy from the sea looked at them with curiosity.

"You must be Bucky," said Ant to the boy.

He looked at Ant sharply. "How did you know my name?"

"We heard the whole story," said Buster. "From the white buffalo…Osiris."

"We found her!" said Sally to Bucky, pointing to the frozen mass of leaves and twigs. "We found Isabella."

"Isabella? But how?"

"These branches are arms," explained Sally. "And this icicle is her nose."

Bucky placed a salt-crusted hand on the ice sculpture. The ice melted under his touch, and the sticks and leaves fell away. As his hand passed through the ice, it was met by another. Golden hair and radiant eyes bloomed before him as the melting ice revealed the face of Isabella.

Freed from her ice prison, Isabella opened her eyes and was reawakened to this world. She looked into the face of Bucky, reached up to the place where his horn had been so cruelly wrested from his body, and traced the scarred tissue.

"Does it hurt?" she asked.

"No," said Bucky through tears, "not anymore."

This made them both smile.

* * *

"Osiris," said Sally, tugging on Buster's coat.

They all turned to the buffalo.

Isabella ran to him. "Father?" She knelt and ran her fingers through his white coat as Bucky and the four extra children formed a circle around his body.

The big brown eyes of the white buffalo flickered with dying fire. "My Isabella," he whispered, "I knew you would come back."

Isabella wept into his mane. "Oh, Father," she cried, "what has happened to us?"

"All is past," he replied. "Look forward, not back."

"Don't go, Father." Isabella wept. "Stay…please stay…"

"I will be with you always…in the Infinite Domain." Osiris wheezed. "It is there that my journey takes me now."

"Father…oh, Father." Isabella wrapped her arms around his wide neck.

"Before I go, a promise you must make," he said.

"Yes, Father, anything."

He struggled to breathe. "Never give her your anger or your hatred—promise me that."

It will be so hard, thought Isabella. *For all the cruelty Hortense wreaks, surely I have a right to hate my sister. But I will honor my father's last wish.*

"Yes, Father, I promise."

"Never, ever…" And on those words, his wide eyes shut for the last time, and his heavy chest was still.

As he let out his last breath, something wondrous and strange happened to the body of Osiris—he turned to wood before their eyes and sprouted a spiraling pole.

The Sea Witch watched from her spiked black seahorse high on the ridge. She saw Isabella weeping over the lifeless body of the old buffalo as it transformed. A screeching cackle peeled from her green lips. With a wave of the hexed horn, she and her seahorse brigade began their furious descent to the shore.

CHAPTER SEVENTEEN

The Horse War

As Ursa neared the old graveyard in the forest, her heart sank. For hours, she had searched the cold woods for Sally, Ant, Buster, and Penny. Now, her worst fears were realized—there, among the stone markers, lay the sleeping bodies of the four missing extra children, their faces dusted with fresh snow.

"Please, God," Ursa prayed, "let it be the sleep from which they wake."

* * *

An ear-splitting cry ripped the air, and all heads turned. A terrible thundering of ten seahorses, led by the Sea Witch, raced down the steep path toward them.

Isabella leaped to her feet. An awful flash coursed through her mind—she had seen this Sea Witch before. In the attic so long ago, it was she who had trapped Isabella in her cocoon of ice. And while Isabella had not aged during her imprisonment on the blighted picture island, she saw that her witch-sister, Hortense, was now very old.

Bucky's heart sank at seeing his horn in the scaly green hand of the Sea Witch. *If only I had stayed in my tank,* he thought to himself, *none of this would have happened.*

"Quick! To the carousel!" shouted Isabella.

They all ran as fast as they could.

Isabella knelt beside one of the broken carousel horses. Brushing sand from its eyes, she laid her hands on the wooden animal.

The rich color returned to the horse's coat, and he was suddenly new again. The wooden horse creaked and then shook, his rear leg kicking the sand. And then he was upright, cold air steaming from his flared nostrils as he let out a neigh.

The extra children could not believe their eyes.

"She is strong, but we are many!" said Isabella, moving to the next carousel horse. Soon, all six of the horses were standing tall on their poles and shuddering with new life.

"Find a horse!" shouted Bucky, helping Penny onto hers. "Hold tight to the poles!"

The shrill screams of the Sea Witch grew louder as she closed in on them.

Ant and Buster each hopped astride dark-brown steeds. Penny's was sand-colored and wore a garland of flowers. A speckled-gray pony knelt so Sally could climb on his back. Isabella mounted her white horse, and Bucky leaped onto a black stallion.

The Sea Witch and her cavalry flew down toward them.

* * *

The black seahorses crashed into the carousel menagerie. Their sharp spines gnawed and chipped the wood of their charmed equestrian adversaries, as balls of ice flew from the Sea Witch's horn. One hit Sally's pony, which bucked and threw her.

"Sally!" yelled Buster, but he could not reach her— the black brigade was upon them.

The Sea Witch rose on her charmed steed and hovered in the air above them. "This island is your prison!" she howled. "The ice will take you all!" She drew circles in the air with the horn, gathering a freezing wind. Black clouds followed her cursed wand, inking the sky.

Bucky's horse lurched and took down one of the seahorses with a strong kick. Penny's colt leaped high in the air and landed on another. Isabella's white horse trampled a third. Seven seahorses remained.

Sally lay in the seagrass. Penny's wooden horse creaked and grew stiff from the frigid air, finally collapsing.

Penny fell with her colt, and they rolled onto the sand. She raced to Sally.

We are down two riders, thought Buster. "It's seven against four!" Buster shouted to Bucky. "The math is not in our favor!"

"No," replied Bucky, his horse rearing up onto its two hind legs. "But magnificence is, my friend! Magnificence is!"

* * *

As the sea eagle flew across the island, she called to her two sons who were diving for cod offshore. Hearing her cry, they sailed across the sky to join her.

* * *

Splintered wood flew from their mounts as Bucky, Isabella, Ant, and Buster fought off the spiked foes. Bucky heard a cry above, and spotted three sea eagles in the sky. Their flight formation reminded him of dolphins, and Bucky recalled seeing dolphins swim in a great circle and surround a school of fish.

And then it dawned on Bucky—*they're from the sea.* "This way!" he shouted to the others. He turned his stallion and headed away from the seahorses.

"We can't give up now!" shouted Ant, not wanting to retreat.

"Trust Bucky!" said Isabella, "He knows these creatures better than we do!" She turned her horse around and quickly galloped behind Bucky.

Ant and Buster followed her.

The sea eagles dropped from the sky, diving toward the shore. Osiris would have to wait—their eyes were trained on the Sea Witch.

Bucky and his team galloped in a wide arc. The seahorses were ferocious, but slower on land, and did not know how to respond. As the carousel horses orbited them, the seahorses clustered in a tight formation. Underwater they were solitary creatures and not used to being in a pack.

The carousel horses, born to travel in an endless wheel, gathered speed. The black steeds closed in on each other, and their spiked backs pricked and bit the adjacent seahorses. The black knot turned on itself as seahorse fought seahorse, for the moment forgetting the ring of wooden chargers surrounding them.

From above, the Sea Witch shot balls of ice that hit Bucky's stallion. The stallion bucked, and Isabella's horse crashed into him. In the chaos, the seahorses began to unknit themselves.

The Witch raised the cursed horn high in the air, preparing to strike.

But the sea eagle and her two sons were upon her, slamming the Sea Witch from behind and knocking her from her horse. As the horn flew from her hand, the sea eagle vaulted to snatch it in her powerful talons. Without the horn, the Sea Witch was helpless against the two remaining birds of prey.

The sea eagle soared to the carousel horses and their riders. From high in the air, she released Bucky's horn. The black seahorses retreated, no longer under the horn's dark magic.

All eyes were on the horn spinning through the air. Through lifting clouds, the whirling spire caught the sun and shot arrows of light. It hurtled through the sky to Bucky, as a ray of golden light peeled from beyond the clouds and struck the horn, fusing it back again to Bucky's forehead.

Robbed of her dark powers, the Sea Witch lay transformed in the sand.

CHAPTER EIGHTEEN

The Carousel

Their vicious leader now defeated, the ten black seahorses slipped back into the surf and disappeared into the dark sea.

Isabella, Bucky, Ant, and Buster jumped down from their carousel horses and rushed to the fallen Sea Witch. Before their eyes, the kelp and seaweed fell away from her, and the green scales that were her skin vanished. What had been the Sea Witch was transformed into the fragile, old body of Miss Bunion, cold and shivering on the sand.

"Where am I?" she whimpered, as if waking from a dream. "What is this place?"

Isabella knelt beside her, taking the old woman's hand into her own. "Oh, Sister, how far time has taken you..."

The shriveled face of Miss Bunion flashed with dreadful recognition. "Ice-a-bella," she said in a brittle voice. She brought a wrinkled finger to Isabella's face. "You are...as you were when I sent you here..." Her words rang with a lifetime of remorse. "What...what have I done?" With Bucky's horn returned to him, all the hate and bitterness that Hortense had carried was evaporated.

"All is past," said Isabella, smoothing the wiry gray hair of her sister. "We must look forward, not back."

Old Miss Bunion shut her eyes tight against the heavy truth of her memories. "Oh, Mother," she whispered to herself, "I missed you too much." She forced open her eyes and stared at those around her. "There is no forgiveness...for what I've done to you, Isabella... and you children, impoverished under my own roof. And you, Narwhal Boy...it was I who took your horn... what has become of you? At my wretched hand?" Miss Bunion wept into the sand, pouring out the sea of wickedness in which she had been drowning all these many years.

"I forgive you," said Isabella.

"And I forgive you," said Bucky.

"Us too," said Buster.

Miss Bunion took Isabella's cheek in her crooked, quaking hand. "So beautiful, I never saw it..." Her voice faded to a whisper. "You shine like the sun..."

Isabella hugged her ancient sister, feeling the life slipping from her.

"Shhh…save your breath, Father is waiting for you in the Infinite Domain."

Isabella laid her sister gently down onto the sand. The body of old Miss Bunion turned to dust before them, and the wind scattered her to the sea.

* * *

Penny sat next to Sally, who was lying in the dune's tall seagrass. Sally had been badly injured in the horse war.

"Did we save Isabella from the witch?" Sally asked.

"Yes—yes we did," said Penny. Sally seemed very tired, and Penny hoped she was not badly hurt.

"Can we go home now?" asked Sally.

"Yes," said Penny.

"Ursa must be worried." Sally's voice was weak.

Having been preoccupied with the transformation of the Sea Witch, the others now rushed to Penny and Sally in the dunes.

"What happened?" said Ant.

"Is she all right?" asked Buster.

"I think so—I don't know," said Penny.

Bucky reached down and took Sally into his arms. "We have to get her back," he said.

"Yes," said Isabella, "to the mirror in the castle."

They hurried to the path beyond the dunes. The horses they had ridden in battle were again wooden and lifeless, standing like sentries, their poles fixed in the sand.

* * *

Osiris had called it the Castle of the Infinite Domain, this towering pillar of black rock, and the extra children had never seen anything so immense. Up the stairs they went, Bucky carrying Sally, to the vast throne room with its chairs made of stone. And at the end of the hall, the mirror that reflected not one's face, but the nature of one's soul.

Before they approached the mirror, Isabella spoke. "Thank you. Your bravery saved me, and it saved No Place Island."

"What will happen when we leave here?" asked Buster.

"The cold will lift, and this island will be returned to a paradise," said Isabella. "And Bucky and I shall reign over it from this Castle of the Infinite Domain."

Penny peered through an arched window in the castle's wall. "Look—the snow is melting," she said.

"The sun has returned," said Bucky. "Soon the plants will be bursting with green leaves again."

"What about the carousel?" asked Ant.

"It will be as new," said Isabella, "and as long as there are children to dream, its animals will turn, and its music will never die."

Sally was tired and nodding off in Bucky's arms.

"Come, we're running out of time," said Bucky.

"To the mirror," said Isabella.

Buster was the first to step up to the glass. "Goodbye," he said to Isabella and Bucky. "I will never forget the adventure we had, or forget you." Instead of showing his own reflection, the surface of the mirror swirled and melted away, revealing white clouds trailing across a blue sky. Buster stepped into it and was gone.

"Goodbye, Isabella, goodbye, Bucky," said Ant. He too approached the mirror and disappeared into the blue sky it revealed.

"I'll miss you, and I'll miss this place," said Penny. And as she entered the mirror, she turned, waving for Sally to follow.

* * *

One by one, Ursa shook the extra children, stirring them back to life. "Buster, Ant, wake up! Sally, Penny, come now!"

Sally fell in and out of sleep; Ursa carried her in her ample arms. "Not this one," Ursa prayed. "Leave this one to us."

As they trudged through the snow, the extra children were shivering and blue from their hours in the cold woods. When they arrived at the Bunion Home, wind was ripping and hissing at the curtains in the attic window. Shards of broken glass splintered the snow below, and there in the wreckage lay the body of old Miss Bunion.

"May God have mercy," whispered Ursa.

The extra children rushed to Miss Bunion's side.

"Poor Miss Bunion," said Penny.

"We forgive you," said Ant, "and Isabella forgives you."

"Look," said Buster, digging out a large ball from the snow. "It's glass…and there's a carousel inside."

"And here's a map," said Penny, peeking into the scrolled canvas which poked up through the snow.

"Children!" cried Ursa, finally catching up to them. "Come away from there! I'll tend to Miss Bunion—go inside and get warm!"

* * *

With the passing of Miss Bunion, everything soon changed at the Bunion Home for Extra Children. Grundy Bunion, who grew more charitable with age, eventually turned over the orphanage to Ursa. She fed and clothed its residents properly, and loved them as if they were her own. And the doors of the Bunion Home opened again as happy children with kind hearts streamed out, into the arms of new parents, new homes, and new lives.

But for now, Sally lay motionless in her bed as Buster, Penny, and Ant kept watch over her. The painted map to No Place Island—"the Place of No Place," as Osiris had called it—lay open on her blanket.

Ant shook the glass dome that Buster had found in the snow next to old Miss Bunion's body. He wound the key underneath, and as the strange music played, Ant took Sally's hand into his own. He traced her finger over the smooth glass.

"Look, Sally," Ant pleaded through his tears, "here's the carousel..." And though her eyes remained closed, he showed Sally the animals stirring up snow inside the dome. "See that one?" He wept, pointing her limp finger at the white buffalo that circled by. "It's Osiris; he's there on the carousel, waiting for us."

But Sally knew this—for she was there, lost in their shared dream, slipping through the Infinite Domain to the world they called the Picture Island.

ACKNOWLEDGMENTS

M any people past and present were part of this book's journey. I'd first like to thank my brother, David, and my sisters Lisa and Shelley, for first discovering Ice-a-bella on a snowy walk by a creek so many years ago. Thanks also to Lisha McDuff and Jody Taylor, two fellow touring musicians who encouraged, read, listened, and drew with me as this book was being written all those years ago when we were on the road together with *Miss Saigon*.

As I revisited this manuscript, my partner, Efrain Cervantes, spurred me to keep going, listened with patience, and provided invaluable guidance. And many thanks to Patrick and Janice Druez, who opened their home for the novella's first public reading. Much gratitude to Lisa Umina and her team at Halo Publishing, for their expertise and wisdom throughout the publication process. I am indebted to Marta Maszkiewicz, as without her evocative drawings, this book would not be complete.

Lastly, I must thank Martin Cowart, whose friendship and heart-centered coaching gave me the courage and belief in myself to imagine this published novella into reality.